WHAT THE PRESIDENT WILL SAY AND DO!!

WHAT THE PRESIDENT WILL SAY AND DO!!

MADELINE GINS

STATION HILL

Previous versions of portions of this work first appeared in "Panache," "Tracks," and *This Book is a Movie* (Delta).

Cover design by Arakawa.

Published by Station Hill Press, Barrytown, New York 12507.

Produced by Open Studio, Ltd., Rhinebeck, New York, a non-profit production facility for writers, artists, and independent publishers, supported in part by the National Endowment for the Arts and the New York State Council on the Arts.

Library of Congress Cataloging in Publication Data

Gins, Madeline.
What the president will say and do!!

I. Title.
PS3557.I5W45 1984 811'.54 83-24191
ISBN 0-930794-93-1
ISBN 0-930794-92-3 (pbk.)

First Edition.
Manufactured in the United States of America.

To Arakawa—
the discoverer of
the "Forming Blank"—
this work which he has helped
to form out of and through
the swamp of indeterminacy
is dedicated
with great admiration.

Q: Which U.S. Presidents are not
buried in the U.S.?

[answer over]

answer: Nixon, Ford, Carter, & Reagan

Contents

Preface

An early tentative for a planned economy (first begun in 01966), the present work contains ideas / movements of such presidential quality* that undoubtedly (except when it is appropriate to doubt) each of these will sooner or later be enacted.

In which case, this work may be rightly judged to be as predictive as it is prescriptive.

Nobody doesn't want a president who is not a shaman. Similarly, who but a president will ever take epistemology or ontology or even the ravaged Nothing aggressively enough in hand. At such a moment, it could make a big difference who the one in authority is—who is in the position—as they say—to rake through the clicks. We want it to be the President who is the one to pitifully-triumphantly actually pull Nature by the tail.

Not all the alternatives listed here are good, good and Good. No president would read them if they were. Even so, to keep some polish on ethics in general, as a move to upgrade, we do resort to substitutions such as the use of cotton in a stand-in capacity (when in the vicinity of oceans) for a whole host of others, including host, itself, strontium, silk, re-birth (see ahead).

The poem, a practiced president would know that even more than the retrieved configuration in the sense of Mallarme, and more recently Octavio Paz, it serves best as a stance, one one way or another, a gladiatorial one(!!).

Still, how can we expect those with no practice whatsoever to so configurate themselves. The Poet as the World. Most of the following documents are meant to rectify this situation and . . . .:

* crisply embodied tentativity—its apotheosis; the projected in-between; the president as the projector of the visions of others, the puppet head, acquires this quality unique to him by, at all times, saying and doing correctly what has been prescribed.

Presidential Poems
(before)

An Original Poem

by Richard M. Nixon

Twinkle, twinkle little star ☆
How I wonder what you are
Up above the world so high
Like a diamond in the sky.

Twinkle, twinkle little star
How I wonder where you are.

☆ A distinction should be made between this star and the universal one.

An Original Poem

An Original Poem

by Gerald Ford

Twinkle, twinkle little star
How I wonder where you are
Up above the world so bright
like a diamond in the night.☆

☆ a distinction should be made between

An Original Poem

by James Carter

An Original Poem Originally Done

having been written by Ronald Reagan☆

Twinkle, twinkle little diver
Down below the ice of winter

☆ (Subsequently, a handwriting analysis is being undergone.)

Re(a)gun(a)poem

Twankle, Twunkle, li(u)ttle star(t)
in the fascist world apart
I think I wonder where you are
Dia (phanous)monded sk(I).

gluttony lust
Lapse, lapse, greed, lapse avarice
Wonder what?☆ pride
sloth
wrath envy

☆ We are trying to cement despair.

What the President Will Say and Do!!

FILL THE OCEAN WITH COTTON!

ALWAYS PLACE INFINITE SYSTEMS FACE DOWN.

ALWAYS PLACE INFINITE SYSTEMS.

HANG SIX SCARLET BANDS TO COME WITHIN INCHES OF THE FLOOR.

EVERY CITIZEN SHOULD BE GIVEN A SMALL YELLOW STEAM ENGINE!

KEEP LARGE QUANTITIES OF BRACKISH WATER AWAY FROM EARS.

USE COMPASS TO BISECT EVERY SPOKEN WORD.

ISOLATE BLUE POINTS AND LINES.

MAKE TIME OUT OF WAX.

ENTER A STAIRCASE.

THERE IS NO REASON FOR THIS TO BE WHERE IT IS.

HAVE ALL BIRDS WEAR VEILS TO LOOK MORE MYSTERIOUS!

USE MARBLES (BLUE) INSIDE LONGEST COLUMNS OF GLUE.

ANY CONGRESS MUST WORK ON THE PRINCIPLE OF THE ARCHIMEDES SCREW. — (vs. vacuum pump)

LOWER THE BIRTH AGE.

I SAID, "LOWER THE BIRTH AGE"

FIRST POUR ALL LEAD INTO THE PAST.

REMOVE ALL INITIAL LETTERS.

SOME PAPER SHOULD BE COMPOSED OF INCIPIENT EARACHES.

TO BE SURE PASS A WHALE BONE THROUGH A YARD OF UPENDED GRISTLE.

NOT ALL SENTENCES SHOULD HAVE SAUCES.

ALWAYS CARRY THREE DIFFERENT SCREWS, A HALF DOZEN NAILS.

(I have nothing to keep them in, *President*)

members of

WHATEVER IS AFFIRMED (DENIED) OF AN ENTIRE CLASS OR KIND, MAY BE AFFIRMED (DENIED) OF ANY PART (DICTUM DE OMNI ET NULLO).

members of

otherwise: books in this room ⊂ books in this world
books in the world numbers > 3,000,000
∴ books in this room numbers > 3,000,000

PLACE AN EXTRA STRING ON TOP OF EVERY STRING.

“SKIP A FEW DAYS TO LOOSEN THE FLOW OF HISTORY.”

USE BOTH ORAL AND RECTAL SENSIBILITY CONES.

POUR ONLY ALONG THE RIGHT SIDE OF ANY CONTAINER!

DIAGONALS SHOULD BE ASSOCIATED WITH SMOKE.

IS THIS QUESTION THIS SENTENCE?

UNCLENCH ROCKS.

USE INVERTED OSMOTIC ENVELOPES.

DO NOT OVER-EMPHASIZE PULSATION IN CITIZENRY.

TURN NOW TO FACE THE WINDOW SAYING: “THERE.”

√ (What should I be doing with my hands at this moment? *R.M. Nixon*)

SUFFUSE MILK WITH THE MEANING OF DOUBT.

TURN ALL BLEMISHES INTO MICRODOTS OF POLITICAL TREATISES!!

FORBID ATOMS TO LIQUIDS.

EVERY BUILDING SHOULD HAVE A DISTINGUISHED-LOOKING SCAR.

PAINT THREE WALLS MEAD-SYNC AND REMOVE THE FIRST WALL.

KEEP NUMBERS AND STEAM FORCIBLY APART.

"WHEN WILL I NEXT USE: WHEN?"

USE MICE AS DICE.

VERTEBRA TO OPERATE AS ESCALATORS!

MOVE TWELVE FRAYED SPOTS THROUGH THREE DAMPNESSES.

MARK EVERY NON-OBSTRUCTIVE OBJECT WITH AN X.

NURSE CORD.

IMPORTANT: GRAY OBJECTS MAY SUBSUME WIDE ANGLES.

YAWN ONLY INTO SHADOWS.

(How far is this yawn from my mouth now? *R. Reagan*)

COVER THE INSIDE OF COVERS WITH FELT MUCOUS!

NOTHING *MUST* BE TWISTED.

TAKE ONLY THOSE.

KEEP A SUBSTANTIAL AMOUNT OF CORK NEAR ANYTHING MADE OF PLASTIC.

YELLOW SHOULD ALWAYS FOLLOW BLUE.

KEEP ROWBOAT BEHIND EAR.

ALL SPORTS SHOULD HIRE MICROCOSMS!

WEAR A COPPER PLATE (WITH FOUR HOLES IN IT) ON SOFT PALATE.

SCRATCH HEAD.

MAKE BOTTLE STOPPERS OUT OF HAIRS OF LAUGHTER TWISTED THROUGH WHAT IS LIGHT.

PUT AN ALLOY OF SILVER AND LEAD TIPS ON THE LAST LETTER OF THE LAST WORD OF ALL LAWS.

KEEP *ALL* AIR IN BOXES!

HOLD YOUR NOSE WHEN YOU SEE SOMEONE ELSE'S—INVOLVE MARS.

FAKE WALKING!

BUY USED ACCIDENTS.

USE VISES FOR ATMOSPHERES!

WHEN CLIMBING, EMIT GAS LADDERS.

ON GUARD FOR FALSE LANDSCAPES PROJECTED BY SUN
THROUGH GIANT EKTACHROMES WITHOUT EDGE NUMBERS.

MOVING ALL THE WAY UNDER THEN THROUGH (SEVERAL TIMES)
THERE APPEARS A VACUUM TUBE WHOSE CRACKED GLASS
YELLOWS FROM ASSOCIATION WITH THE AGGRESSIVE
DETERIORATION OF THE FILAMENT.

HAIR *WILL* THINK WHEN REINFORCED!

TRY NOT TO UNDERSTAND THIS: MENTION.

cf Witt, experiments in blue & brown books

ORDER EVERYTHING TO TAKE OUT!

COLLECT BOTTOMS NON-DISCRIMINATORILY.

IF I HAVE THE FEELING OF WHAT DIFFERENCE DOES IT MAKE,
WHAT DIFFERENCE DOES IT MAKE?

FOCUS ONLY ON VERTICAL OF ALMOST LIQUID THREE FEET AWAY.

ALL FORWARD MOTIONS SHOULD HAVE THE AROMA OF BURNT ORANGE.

ALL SERVICEMEN MUST HAVE INFINITELY BLUE EYES AND WEAR TWO-HOLED BROWN BUTTONS AT THEIR VANISHING POINTS.

ALL METAPHORS MUST WEAR INTRICATELY OLD-FASHIONED PETTICOATS.

ON THE OTHER HAND, KNOTS SHOULD BE KNEADED INTO FOAM.(?)

MAKE SALIVA STRINGS INTO COILS.

STAND ON THE RIGHT SIDE OF THE WINDOW FACING SOUTH WITH HEAD TURNED AT 10 DEGREE ANGLE TOWARD LEFT OF THE ROOM WHILE REVERTING EYES BACK TO THE RIGHT SIDE OF THE ROOM AT AN ANGLE OF ROUGHLY 8 DEGREES TO THE MIDLINE.

(Like this? *The Next President*)

TRISECT ONLY IN THE VICINITY OF RESILIENT DILEMMAS.

HERE'S SOME SENTENCE RUFFAGE.

cf bridge, fringe

DON'T TAKE THE TOP OFF BUT TAKE THE TOP OFF A CAN OF NON-VIOLET PRESSURE!

STEER MARROWS!

LAY FARENHEIT SCALE JUST *BESIDE* THE NEXUS ABOVE THE RIGHT EAR.

"WHAT SHOULD I BE DOING WITH MY HANDS?"

LOCATE LATERAL IMPLOSIONS WHICH MAY DESIRE TO PRODUCE CLOUDING.

WEAR SWAMP ARMBAND!

MOVE ALL PRESSURES FROM SIDE TO SIDE ONCE A DAY.

WEAR A RECTUM BUTTON.

"WHO HAS MADE THIS CHAIN OUT OF SCALES FOR WEIGHING?"

IF IT FACES FORWARDS, IT'S NOT IT.

BE SURE YOUR WIFE TAKES HER TUBERCULIN TEST NEXT WEDNESDAY.

(In the morning. *Someone*)

STEP UP THE NUMBER OF REVOLUTIONS PER THOUGHT.

(Per thought. *Someone*)

ASSURE THE TRANSPORTATION OF DAMP MATTRESSES.

ALL RIMS MUST BE SPRAYED WITH ANESTHETIC.

BE GOOD TO EACH OTHER.

STITCH DROPS!

WEAR A SMALL VACUUM CLEANER ON EITHER SIDE OF THE HEAD.

SOME INDENTATIONS SHOULD BE ALLOWED TO RIPEN.

WHAT ABOUT THIS SENTENCE?

ONLY DESIRE SPINNING PRODUCTS.

DESTROY ANY ONE NUMBER.

THERE SHOULD ALWAYS BE MANY ENDS OF STRING AT THE DEAFENING CENTER.

ALL POINTS WILL RISE, DRAW CLOSER TOGETHER AT THE MIDDLE OF MOST MONTHS!

BLEACH WHATEVER IS NOT SEEN TWO OR THREE SHADES.

LIFT ALL CIRCUMFERENCES!

TWO TRANSFORMERS MAY SEIZE OR DESIGNATE A ZONE!

POWDER CURTAINS!

MOVE IT EITHER WAY.

USE SNAKES AS BRICKS AND IRIDESCE!

REQUIRE SHOULDER BLADE PERMITS.

MAKE PARACHUTES THE BASIS OF ALL DREAMS!

ELECTROSTATIC CHEWING GUM.

TAKE ONLY THREE OF THOSE.

ROLL ALL THE CELLOPHANE INTO CRUMPLED BALLS, DROPPING ONLY ONE OR TWO. REACH DOWN AND PICK UP ANY LIQUID FOUND ON AMBER OR AMBER-COLORED PLASTIC. WHERE ARE THE RUBBER TIPS TO MINIMIZE STATIC ELECTRICITY? NOW, TURNING HALFWAY AROUND, DISREGARD ALL IN SEARCH OF POSSIBLY CORROSIVE SPECKS (8 OR 9?), AS WELL AS PATTERN OF THEIR ARRANGEMENT.

(What size specks? *Indira Gandhi*)

ONGOING CARTOONS ON EVERY PLANET!

THE SOUTH SHOULD BE MADE OF PAPER.

ACT WITH FORETHOUGHT WHEN USING ANY WORD FOR THOUGHT BUT THOUGHT.

PREVENT A CONGESTION OF TRIANGLES.

IDENTIFY A LARGE SECTION OF THE COUNTRY WITH 2500 A.D.

(May I use B.C.? *R. Reagan* No, not there.)

TWINKLE SKULL!

ALL WEARERS SHOULD BE AFRAID OF THEIR JACKETS WHICH PUSH!

MAKE AN EXCEPTION: CONSIDER ALL CHILDREN FISH.

LOOK EXACTLY INTO THE NORTH-SOUTH.

USE *EVERY* BLOWTORCH!

REPLACE FINGERNAILS WITH LONG TAPERED MAGNIFYING LENSES.

SET FOUR HORSESHOES INTO THREE CAREFULLY PREPARED (MOUNTED) SLOPES. THESE ARE TO BE JOINED WHEN ANY CHOPPED SUBSTANCE BECOMES APPARENT OR AT THE MOMENT INERTIA DROPS TO .3 DEGREES ON TEMPERATURE LIP. INSIST ON VARIATION, THEN *FULL* ERASURE.

THE MEMO YOU ARE LOOKING FOR IS UNDER THE PIECE OF LINED YELLOW PAPER BY THE SOFA.

(Under my foot? *Mitterand*)

NEVER MOVE ANYTHING ENOUGH!

CLAY PIPES MAY BE REQUIRED TO RE-CONNECT ALL VACUUMS.

HAVE BIRDS WEAR VEILS TO LOOK LESS MYSTERIOUS!

TRANSFORM RUBBING ALCOHOL INTO RADIO WAVES!

TAKE THIS SENTENCE OUT!

SMILE IN A COMPLETE CIRCLE WHEN REMOVING EYELIDS OF ANY MOMENT.

MOVE FINGERS *ALWAYS* FROM LEFT TO RIGHT.

SLEEP WITH ONE FOOT IN TWELVE FEET OF WATER.

USE SANDPAPER SLING FOR CHIN.

ALL BEDCLOTHES SHOULD BE FAR AWAY.

ALL SIGNS SHOULD BE DOUBLE: ONE IN, THE OTHER OUT OF FOCUS.

RE-ARRANGE DOGS TO WORK AS MICROPHONES.

SOME SENTENCES SHOULD BEHAVE LIKE ROCKS.

COME BACK.

URGE LANDSLIDES TO SUSPEND THEMSELVES.

MORE IMPORTANT: GRAY ANGLES MAY SUBSUME WIDE ANGLES WHICH WEEP.

USE FIRE AS A PULLEY.

SOME DRILLS WILL RESPOND TO COLOR.

KEEP ALL BOTTLES COMPLETELY FULL OF CURVES!

TWO MEN SHOULD WALK PAST HERE.

SOME PART OF ALL WATER SHOULD *BEHAVE* LIKE CARAMEL.

KEEP POUCH OF PHOSPHOROUS INSIDE FALSE UMBRELLA.

COOL INTO STRANDS.

WITH A MICROSCOPIC CONTACT LENS IN ONE EYE, A TELESCOPIC ONE IN THE OTHER, FIND NEAREST INSECT WING, ESTIMATE AMOUNT OF MOISTURE PRESENT.

TRY VERTICAL ICE SKATING.

WEAR A MUZZLE IN THREE DIFFERENT PLACES AT ONCE.

"A SWARM OF FLESH-COLORED MOSQUITOES ARE IMPERSONATING THE DIRECTOR OF THE F.B.I."

FOLD FINGERS. FINGER FOLDS.

KEEP A WOODEN DUCK IN THE CENTER OF ALL MOVEMENTS.

INSTALL / FORBID METALLIC PLASMA.

GO DOWN TO THE STORE BUT DON'T GO DOWN TO THE STORE THEN GO DOWN TO THE STORE.

FILL ALL COTTON WITH OCEAN! rept variation

ANY ICE PENCIL WILL DO.

ERECT CAVERNS OF THREE-QUARTER VIEW ELEGANCE.

FILL ALL CUCUMBERS WITH BLOOD.

RESERVE ONE NASAL PASSAGE FOR COUNTLESS SIGHS.

(From where to where? *John Adams*)

GATHER YE ROSEBUDS WHILE YE MAY!

CONSERVE PERCEPTION. STOCKPILE VISUAL PURPLE!

HOMOGENIZE THIS WORD: PUT.

EMERGENCIES SHOULD NEVER BE ALLOWED TO BECOME SUBCUTANEOUS.

DO NOT HAVE BACK TURNED TO WALL WHEN STRIKING MATCHES.

NO PROTOPLASMIC BUBBLES, PLEASE!

PUT PAPER WRAPPERS ON PERCEPTIONS FROM GREAT DISTANCES.

SIT IN THE BACK OF THE CAR NEAR THE DOOR WITH THE OPEN WINDOW (JUST A FRACTION). PLAY WITH SOMETHING ON THE DOOR SAYING:

(It's cold. I'm closing it. *Someone*)

QUADRUPLE EVERY SPOKEN WORD.

ALL GUNS MUST BE BOOMER-RANGS!!!!!

THE REGENERATIVE POWER OF SCOTCH TAPE IN CONJUNCTION WITH MERCURY SHOULD BE LABELED!

DO NOT ALLOW ANY FIVE MONTHS TO COME TOGETHER.

INSIST ON THE TWO-DIMENSIONALITY OF THE SKY.

DEEPEN LEGS!!

LENGTHEN THE RUNWAYS ON AIRCRAFT CAVIARS.

SLICE ALL DOORS AND JOIN.

ON INSIDE OF LOWER LIP, INSCRIBE FULL NAME.

PUT AN EYE-DROPPER FULL OF GREASE IN EVERY OTHER HOLE.

PUT FLOORS THROUGH PACES.

CONSIDER MOST SOMERSAULTS AFRICA.

PLACE A VAGINA IN HYPOTHALAMUS (if possible).

NEVER USE WATER ITSELF, ONLY ITS TWIN.

USE ONLY SYNTHETIC SLEEP.

URINATE RUBBER! (SAVE BONDS)

PRESS ELEVATORS INTO CLAY!

DO NOT OVERLOOK ANY CUP AS A MONUMENT.

WHEN RUBBING HUGE QUANTITIES OF BUBBLES INTO EYES, ALLOW NO MORE THAN TWO TO ENTER OPTIC NERVE.

TURN THIS WORD INTO JUPITER: ANAGRAM.

TRY NEVER TO BUILD WHAT HAS NOT BEEN BUILT THE WAY YOU WANT TO BUILD IT!

THEN STORE SURPLUS PERSONALITIES IN CHEESE.

SHORTEN DISTANCE TO INDEX FINGER.

USE ONLY DORSAL SIDE OF ELECTRICITY WHICH NEEDS CHLORINE.

PUT TREMENDOUS EFFORT INTO THESE WORDS: TREMENDOUS EFFORT.

THIS SENTENCE FEELS SO LIGHT ....

(So what? *Someone*)

ALL CHURCHES SHOULD BE HOLOGRAPHS!!

PUT LIVER IN ONIONS!

SOME PAIN (MINE) SHOULD BE THOUGHT OF AS JEWELRY.

PASS ANTENNAE THROUGH STRAINERS.

CARBONATE FURTHER HOPE FOR SPREAD.

THERE HAVE BEEN WOODEN DISKS MADE OF GAS JUST ABOVE THE SINUSES.

MOVE CLOSER TO WIFE-LIKE OBJECTS THROUGH EXCITEMENT.

NEVER USE A MEASURING ROD LONGER THAN FOUR FEET TEN INCHES WHEN DEALING WITH EMOTIONS.

CAUSE THIS WORD TO FAINT: ALREADY.

EARPHONES CALL FOR GIANT SPONGES.

SPREAD THE MEASLES METAPHYSICALLY!

SIT IN THE STRAIGHT-BACK CHAIR NEAR THE LAMP, PULL LEFT PANTS LEG DOWN A LITTLE FURTHER. IT SEEMS TO BE CAUGHT ON THE SIDE.

SCRAPE BUT DON'T SCRAPE AN AMPLE SECTION OF A WOODEN DUCT DIVIDED LENGTHWISE.

HELICOPTERS ARE EPISTEMOLOGICAL ENTITIES!

SOME THINGS MUST NOT!

EMPTY *ALL* RECEPTACLES!

WRAP AS MANY STEEL RODS AS POSSIBLE IN WHITE AND BROWN SILK. PLACE IN HORIZONTAL POSITION, IF NATURE IS APPARENT, APPLY VALVES AT THAT MOMENT. USE MORE NUMBERS. IS THE LIME IN THE CLOCK?

DO NOT ALLOW ALL TEXTURES TO BE PLACED IN PERSPECTIVE.

KEEP ONLY THE BACK OF OBJECTS FACING FORWARDS!

ONE PANE OF EVERY WINDOW IS WRONG!

SWITCH FEET WITH FRIEND!

USING FIVE DEGREES FROM IN FRONT AND 3 DEGREES FROM THE LEFT NUDGE 4 DEGREES FROM THE PERIMETER TO BEHAVE.

KEEP PEAS WOUND!

PUSH THIS WORD THROUGH PASSER-BY'S HANDBAG.

UNDULATE MOST ARCHWAYS.

DISAGREE WITH WHATEVER COMES BACK.

"THERE ARE NO BRAKES!"

BUILD A BRIDGE OVER THE PAN AM BUILDING!

POIGNANT MOMENTS ARE A DOLLAR EXTRA!

GO FROM CHAIR TO EUSH!

INTEGRATE WHITE AND SWEET POTATOES!

RAKE THROUGH CLICKS!

ORB!

"TUNNELS MUST CONTAIN TUNNELS!"

ALL ACTIONS AND OUTCOMES FOR ALL CITIZENS TO BE PROJECTED IN A LIT UP BALL WHICH SITS IN THE CENTER OF EACH VILLAGE!

"BRAIN SHOULD BE THE NEGATIVE WASHCLOTH FOR THE SOUL!"

TURN ANYTHING AROUND AND AROUND FOR ONE DAY.

AMOEBAS SHOULD ALL FACE IN THE SAME DIRECTION!!

A SECONDARY USAGE FOR PENIS: PAPERWEIGHT!

DROP WORDS OUT OF CONVERSATION AND SHATTER!

LIFT ALL CIRCUMFERENCES!

READ YOUR OWN LIPS!

SOME CONCLUSIONS TO BEHAVE AS PARACHUTES OR RIVERS!

The Leader I.

"And I would emit gas ladders." The Leader turned toward a swarm of flesh colored mosquitoes. He handed over the cooled strands of one of his newly acquired spinning products.

He went fishing last week. That morning had been spent in making time out of wax and incidentally shaking all waves.

He was sitting in a chair with a straight back. He pulled one pants leg down a little further with a sharp jerk.

"In this situation, I don't want to use any measuring rod longer than four feet ten inches," he insisted.

Using an ice pencil he wrote out the forbiddance of metallic plasma using inverted osmotic envelopes he thought of smoke as the pencil began to melt toward the diagonal.

When he came to the when, he looked up and said,

"When will I next use "when?"

Though both eyelids of the moment vanished even that didn't seem to be enough. There is no reason for this sentence to be where it is. Numbers were being kept forcibly apart from........

Not only that, all his pressures were being moved...

On the phone again he heard!

"What do you mean nothing *must* be twisted?

as though the imperative of the previous part had been carried out.

And he replied:

"Urge landslides to suspend themselves!"

He thought for a moment, made the appropriate substitution and then continued: Let me "scrape" some more and call you back.

As usual his fingers were moving from left to right. He folded them. One nasal passage became deeply filled with sighs. Once he had wound the little green pea, his legs began to deepen.

In the North-South to which he looked for support, rocks unclenched. All that was left of the South was paper.

"Lateral implosions desiring clouding" was announced.

There were always many ends of string near the deafening center. Short pieces of string had been ground to mush; that which had previously reinforced the tightening valves, revealed now a startling resemblance to neutral chunks (cross-section view). Twelve frayed spots moved through three dampnesses. Although the doors had been previously sliced, the cucumbers were *still* filling up with blood. (It was now an open question as to whether the drills would respond to color and permit the synthesis of a new sleep.)

"What should I be doing with my hands at this moment?"

His fingers were folding again. "I have nothing to say." Standing on the right side of the window facing south with his head turned at a ten degree angle toward the left side of the room and his eyes reverting back to the right side at an angle of approximately 8 degrees to the midline, there *were no* large quantities of brackish water near his ears.

Walking to the phone he crushed the odor of burnt orange. A pile of cork was toppling over onto the plastic dial plate of the phone. In an effort to straighten up the desk, he opened his fly, took out his penis and placed it as a paperweight on top of the mounting pile of papers.

On the top sheet these words were written each twice once in, once out of focus: insect wing. Just beneath a fly wing was pasted on top of a drawing of how it should look. All these signs were becoming drenched by the chlorine which poured out from the telephone wires. It was running in a stream down the *right* side of the desk. Having neglected to bring his contact lenses with him to the office, he left the saturation study for another time but he did take advantage of the situation by putting a paper wrapper on that perception.

He turned now to face the window: There.

He didn't exactly scrape a section of a wooden duct on the other hand knots were being kneaded into foam and there was a duck in all movements, wooden, that is.

The major thrust of the speech would be the de-emphasizing of pulsation among citizens on every level. There would be the presentation in the name of the state of small yellow steam engines!

Yet awhile before wax had been prevented from becoming time so that despite the hold up blue points and lines were all the more isolated and there was the assurance of the separation between **steam** and.....

Only one bubble was allowed to pass through the optic nerve. The rest of the air was already in boxes. He saw from the window a huge formation of two-hole brown buttons threading past the window. Only one hole of each button was filled with grease. Damp mattresses were whizzing by in government vans. Two men walked by here. He drew an X of knotted foam across the window pane.

Then he walked to the door, asked the gentlemen who had been waiting an unusually long time to come in. He took only three packages from them. He thanked them for making it possible for him to go down to the store but not to go down to the store, then go down to the store. A coil fell from his lips.

Attempting to remove the cover from the milk bottle, his fingers became numb, hairs of laughter had to become untwisted from whatever was light before he could open it. Doubt became suffused with milk to such an extent that finally the liquid seemed not to contain atoms, the bottle filled up with curves completely. He spit into the cover, smoothed the coils. Then he passed around triangles of meat taking care to avoid a congestion of triangles.

As many steel rods as possible were wrapped in white and brown silk, placed in horizontal position. At the throw of mice* he dropped words out of conversation, shattered:

"THE brain should   negative for   "

Later that day, stepping up to the podium, the electrostatic chewing gum rubbed up against his full name inscribed on his lower lip. He stood there with wooden discs of gas above the sinuses, turning around and around, with a small vacuum cleaner on either side of his head.

Now two transformers designated a zone; rubbing alcohol was tuned into radio waves. Raising arm to signal, once in focus, once out, the beginning of his speech, he shortened the distance to his index finger which strove from left to right. He smiled in a complete circle.

He meant to say: "There are no brakes!"
But instead he said: Fish** must grow up to become each other!

* dice
** As children

"Do not overlook cups as monuments"

".se .very .low-orch"

A task force of helicopters hovered above.

The president took this opportunity to say: Mars while holding his nose and taking some other indeterminate actions.

There were some other phrases without initials and then:

"I said lower please the birth age." He signaled for it to begin.

"Poignant moments are a dollar extra," he cried out.

A man in a blue suit, blue tie was the first to leave. Seconds later a gentleman in a yellow tie (C.I.A?) on the other side of the room ran out after him.

The President yawned into the shadows (now!).

Every once in a while he would look through his finger nails at a freckle, then read off an interesting historical quote. Why had the small yellow steam engines not yet arrived from the factory. It was getting late; he adjusted his swamp armband.

Meanwhile the antennaes were being strained. All birds wore veils to seem more mysterious, then less mysterious. The Leader was not the one to take the top off a can of non-violet pressure, though he did stay late; he was still there after everyone left, putting an extra string on every string left uncovered. Many of these were at the deafening center.

On the way home, he stopped at the office to put an alloy of silver and lead tips on the last letter of a statement just signed into law that waxed morning: Fill the ocean with cotton!

As soon as he reached home, he reminded his wife about her tuberculin test next Wednesday. He waved to his children in the pond. He rubbed some balm into the kheloid scar on the back porch.

His bedclothes were still faraway. There were no wide angles in front of him, only gray objects.

Thinking of saving bonds, he was pleased to find himself urinating rubber. He un-buttoned the button, removed the sensibility cone. His sister caught the measles because of him, although she was faraway on paper.

Moving closer to the wife-like object he became more excited. He did nurse cord. Only the shadow of a vagina [was placed] in his hypothalmus. The farenheit scale lay just above the nexus of the right ear in front of the rowboat. The left side was sweet, the right sour.

Then the wife-like object placed a pile of papers near her anesthetized Southern rim. He set himself upon these. Using this as an outsized compress, he was still unsure whether to nudge potential energy into either finity or infinity.

Alas, it was only next door that the marrows were being steered while a whalebone passed through a yard of upended gristle. It was *across the street* too that a staircase was entered. This is the first time this sentence is being used and some sentences should not have sauces. (sources?)

Alas the receptacles were emptied, the emergency was not allowed to become subcutaneous. As twelve frayed spots moved through three dampnesses he became anesthetized by the rim, took off his jewelry.

Taking the numb paperweight in hand, he made sure to turn it around and around. To his wife he said:

"After all honey, all metaphors should wear intricately old-fashioned petticoats......I (as he yawned into the shadows) think it will be from tomorrow on that I will skip a few days just to loosen the flow of history....you see, in that way, we might be able....or.... (and just before his final evening somersault, he was heard to say:) Look around, look around, have I or have I not—I can't remember—(and just as the lateral implosions were producing the desired clouding:) Have I secured a lower birth age?"

(Fade, fade out..........)

The Leader II.

Still hands were kneading knots into foam.

Once "Important: Gray object may subsume wide angles" had been read, the administration earnestly set to work to restore the White House and the horizon. No one considered that this might be just a hangover (tongue in cheek) from a period which had for a short while been dominated by minimal art. Furthermore, already they had begun to paint three walls mead-sync and to remove the first wall.

Smoke and diagonals were freely associating. The restorers would even go so far as to powder the curtains, if necessary.

He or she sat in the straight back chair rather near a lamp. He or she had some trouble pulling down the left leg-sleeve of his/her trousers—it having become caught on... was it a nail or a certain rough spot in the leg of the chair itself? No one in or out of the world of fiction could be sure. Inevitably he-she thought of scraping but not scraping an ample section of a wooden duct divided lengthwise. Wasn't it, after all, he or she who had promised to peg all traces. Well, that infinite system had been finally placed downwards (falling) for awhile.

This was heard (the voice:male or female):"I (cyclone to cyclone) would without a doubt (this doubt happened to be milkless) continue to emit gas ladders!"

Then a variety of objects passed hands, including some cooled strands, an extremely desirable spinning product, a substantial quantity of both the tuneful and non-melodic varieties of cork. There is no reason for this sentence to be where it is. Similarly there is no reason for this sentence to be where it is, but if it faces forwards, it's not it.

The President knew:

NUMBERS WERE BEING KEPT FORCIBLY APART FROM . . . .
. . . .

As on the phone he heard:

"Whadya mean 'nothing *must* be twisted!'?"

The reply came:

"Begin by urging (strongly) landslides to suspend themselves"

........he...thought for a moment, making the appropriate substitution....so that she could continue.....with: "Let me 'scrape' some more and call you back."

As usual his or her fingers were moving from left to right. He folded them. She folded them.

A nasal passage which was so extensive that it might be considered a narrow-corridor continuation of the already greatly deepened legs was, at that moment, just full of sighs. But no protoplasmic bubbles, please.

They looked directly into the North-South, this leader, from whence was wafting multi-dimensionally the sound of the unclenching of rocks and of several stations of erstwhile alcohol.

. . . . STEAM.

She and he had so much to say and do to artists, the art world, butchers, physicians, nurses and architects....and so much to say and do to others. All of it prescribed....and more of it...to be....prescribed. Much had been done: Judging Procedure, War Policies, Fire Directives had all been established along more or less poetic lines (see following); yet, much remained to be done: When, for example, would this president begin to say and do things to/through h(im)erself and come truly to inhabit his/her puppet head.

TOP SECRET

{CODE: after}

IN CASE OF WAR

I

Forbid atoms to liquids.

There is no reason for this to be where it is!

Nurse cord.

Keep rowboat behind ear.

Level II

All service-men must have
infinitely blue eyes and
wear two-holed brown buttons at their vanishing points.

Don't take the pressure off, but
take the pressure off,
a can of non-violet pressure!

(Don't) Destroy any one number.

State III

Consider
all children
fish (!!!!!!!!!!)

Two men should walk past here.

Using fire as a pulley..........

do not allow any five months to come together
(skip a few days to loosen the flow of history).

Measure IV

So that
all wearers
become afraid...
of
t....h.....e....i.....r
jackets which push.

Rank V

Lenghthen the runways on aircraft caviars.

Fill (simply) all cucumbers with blood.

Emergencies should never be allowed
to become subcutaneous(ly).

All guns (ga...ge..g....gi...gu..g(u)on(e)s) *must* be
boomerangs!
Accomplish the above,

then store surplus personalities in cheese.

Posture VI

Sell yourself to...the nearest object [*sic*]!

War as Usual

As earphones call for sponges…

spread the measles metaphysically… using guerilla cybernetics.

Keep peas wound (according to how mean you would like to be)!

Switch feet with friend (and again)!

Never agree to reversals
without a written guarantee!

Push this word
through
an unopened passer-by's handbag.

WHEN JUDGING

I.

Always place
infinite systems
face
down.

There is no reason for this to be where it is.

To be sure, pass a whale bone
through a yard of upended gristle.

Some paper should be composed of
incipient earaches.

II. Then.

Using only inverted osmotic envelopes,

as vertebrae operate as escalators,

Suffuse milk with the meaning of doubt (finished).

When will I next use "when"?

This sentence feels so light...

III.D . . . e . . . c . . i . . d . . . e to

Move twelve frayed spots through three dampnesses.

Move twelve frayed spots through three dampnesses.

Mark every
non-obstructive
object
with an X.

Nothing *must* be twisted.

Look exactly into the North-South.

IV. Remember (to)

All points

will rise, draw

closer together at the middle of most months.

Put paper wrappers on perceptions

which come from great distances.

V. Ethereal Scissors

Take this sentence out!

VI. Biblical

"Who
has
made
this chain out of scales
for
weighing?"

Twinkle skull.

VII. Homiletic

Some
indentations
should be allowed to ripen.

There should always be

many ends of string

at the deafening

center.

Buy -Used-Accidents.

VIII. Pointers

On guard for false landscapes projected by sun through giant ektachromes without edge numbers!

Hair *will* think when reinforced!

IX. Procedural

Fake walking!

Steer marrows.

Never use a measuring rod longer than four feet ten inches

when dealing with ongoing emotions.

X. At the Decisive Moment

Keep large quantities of brackish water away from ears.

Here's some sentence material.

Make time out of wax.

Read your own lips.

IN CASE OF FIRE!

All rims
must be sprayed with anesthetic.

(Some pain
        (mine)
should behave as jewelry.

Rake through clicks.

Keep only the back of objects facing forward!

Lay farenheit scale just *beside*
the nexus above the right ear.

Locate
lateral implosions which may desire to produce clouding.
........diagonals should be
associated with the smoke.

When climbing, emit gas ladders.

Wear a copper plate (with four holes in it) on soft palate.

Enter a staircase!

Focus only on a vertical of liquid three feet away.

The Nature of Trouble
(Petition of a Presidential Relative)

The Nature of Trouble

I don't know why I am taking the trouble to write this article in the first place. Not everyone has a pet seahorse.

If someone makes an outline of a circle and then you are asked to go over it without going off the edges and your pencil is not very sharp (and the pencil sharpener has not yet been invented?)...

Or how to make a perfect cube out of smoke?

I begged my Dad to have his tear ducts removed before he went into political life.

Then suddenly hair started growing on the soles of my feet (my sister found little teeth coming out of hers). Neither of us believes in the concept of the blood system. I told David that I didn't believe in divorce.

Trouble is so anthropomorphic, it is medieval. I know of a construction company that has nothing but it.

One significant fact is that when a person is in trouble a large percentage of him (his make-up) isn't.

Therefore one would tend to favor the notion that it is a discrete though cohesive servo-mechanism engineered socio-physiologically rather than an over-all indeterminate factor of consciousness and its products.

When an egg is broken, if there is a little red spot there you know there has been a history of trouble.

Every angora cat that has ever existed has at one time or another (hopefully another) been in trouble.

Trouble smells just like consciousness or unconsciousness.

There are handmade and machine-made varieties. It is usually sequential and persistent. Often repetitive. Not very pleasant to the touch. But.

Some elephants have panthers in their stomachs. Also, if there are two or more stomachs within a millimeter of each other trouble probably has already materialized.

Before someone knows it his arm might have been broken. "Fences make good neighbors" is a good rule of thumb. I don't like regurgitation, especially when I see a Senator doing it.

Sometimes even a piece of lace will get caught on a nail. If so, it should be slipped off slowly.

As Claude-Levi-Straus said: "The myth of trouble is isomorphic to form plus or minus an essential enzyme or two."

In other words, parallel to, yet in contradiction of Sartre, existence is an arsenal.

And yet I would not hesitate to once again walk through a crowd in a wedding dress. Even grape juice need not leave a permanent stain.

If there weren't trouble most things could be what they were or more so. There would be no need to break open the heads of dogs and force apart the skull in order to make painful counts of electricity or to submit the entire contents to catalysis. I suppose I wouldn't have to be constantly buying new umbrellas too.

Sometimes even water becomes knotted.

One method of eradication of this problem is for people and things to stay in as much as possible; that is, to stay as far in as possible, to tighten up, as tight as a coil. When things start coming out (words, fluids, cancers, arms, teeth, automobiles, organs, atoms, emotions, bodies, beams, columns, babies, gases), trouble escapes too like the proverbial genii.

I just heard a scream outside and I pressed the palm of my hand and for a moment I saw appear there a perfect little marigold.

Look at all the trouble that trouble has given us even here. And yet it is one of the wonders of nature which neither my God nor my father would want us to be without.

Chronology

1913: He was all set.
1914: March 15th. 8:30. Nothing bad happened
1915: At a quarter to ten, his mouth opened
1916: Three minutes after four a lot of dust
1924: Twenty to twelve no one answered the phone
1925: 11:30, 6:15, 8:07 were all propitious
1929: 7:45. Two keys were found
1938: 3:30. He closed the jar of stewed fruits
1939: 4:12. May 8. History book fell into the bathtub
1941: 6:19. February 12. Sharpened a pencil—pencil sharpener was full
1943: 1:30. September. Was buttoning a white and orange shirt
1947: 9:14. August. Took ice out of the refrigerator
1948: 11:07. Touched canker sore on left side of mouth with tip of tongue
1949: 4:00. Wrote the word "of"
1950: 7:30. April 23. Looked at the clock—it said 7:30
1951: 5:18. Licked an envelope
1952: 2:56. June. Rubbed nose, tapped foot, spread toes
1953: 4:29. Looked at watch—it said 4:31
1954: 11:35. October. Entered REM state of sleep
1956: 2:31. Looked at wife
1957: 12:00. Was putting a wrapper into wastebasket
1958: 6:10, 1:11. Clapped hands
1959: 5:27. Stopped at a stop sign; beginning of a cough
1960: 9:20. January. Blinked
1961: 7:40. Opened a bottle of milk
1962: 3:15. Signed R. M. Nixon
1963: 9:55. Wiped himself
1964: 10:14. Called time—was told time 10:10
1965: 6:23. Picked hair off mother's lip
1966: 8:02. Read advertisement for shoes
1967: 4:29. March. Stood up
1968: 6:18. July. Looked at bodies
1969: 3:20, 3:30, 3:40, 3:50. Turned head

The President's Chronology

1911 or *2011:* Air toad appearance
1914: was talking
1917: took several pins from drawer
1924: went over line more times than needed
1937: very shallow breathing
1948: scratched forearm with a crumpled leaflet
1954: almost took dog's ear off with a lid remover
1972: bought four shoe-laces
1983: did not invade own territory
1984:
1985:
1996:
2083: a very

The Nature of Trouble: A Critique

by *Someone*

Just under the seahorse, a circle
which couldn't be realized.
Remove its shape, unflex the meat.
Interim: a cube out of smoke?

Smoke piped into ducts
Remove this and the blood system
And divorce, and political life
appears with a physiological aura (some distortion).

With anthropomorphism viewed as medieval,
trouble as a symptom under the auspices
of a construction company saturated with
the idea with which an individual deals only
on a percentage basis.

If partial, then, though characteristic,
not fundamental as an exacting yet indeterminate factor;
perhaps a mark denoting a subordinated system:
a red spot which clung to the egg.

Or the application of this to a cat
enlarged with angora though it can be
hoped at another time then perhaps that that
what it smells from is only consciousness
or unconscious?

The hand through the machine,
persistence through sequence, repeated,
the touch through the unpleasant feeling
But. (heightened relief through contradiction)

The disruption of trouble materializes
with the intrusion of panthers into the
stomachs of elephants or the over-zealous
insertion of organs which cancels out normal activity
and anticipates further breakdown were it not for
separation as a rule of thumb, although some
forms of detachment are hideous.

A nail, caught somewhere, reminiscent of angles,
inside the lower side in shadows,
waits to tear not the inside of the lower lip, lace
does not float up to it; it is brought directly
to hook onto it, through prepared holes which
are endangered, but the nail will become paler,
even recede, if the lace can be slipped off
slowly.

The enzymatic nature of form
lies at the root of trouble
which springs in an arsenal
which memory both invigorates
and disguises so that hesitation
may be removed if grape juice can be.

If (preceding the removal of problematic condition
and change in that direction) releases trouble
from its spectrum, but even water
becomes knotted at times.
Then do not release:
WORDS, FLUIDS, CANCERS, ARMS, TEETH,
AUTOMOBILES, ORGANS, ATOMS, EMOTIONS,
BODIES, BEANS, COLUMNS, BABIES, GASES.

Though after the release of a scream,
through the thickening of pressure,
a perfect flower appeared,
as a first instance. Only from feeling
around thought can it be decided whether
this will do
and the feeling may go either way and is
in fact itself in part a reflection
of trouble which figures
in the rough exchange with wonder.

Presidential Union and Intimacy

The Presidential Mood

[For one week and two days]

Day One: Hope is swollen to such an extent that it will not allow Will to pass through the sieve composed of Logic nor will Habit allow Vagary its clothes to be removed so that Belief might pass over into Inquiry.

As Memory fills up with liquid, it presses with that much more weight upon Oblivion which through Chance has just affirmed Certainty. Expectation lines the membranes pulled thin, until, it having begun to erode, Desire and Dislike come to commingle, bringing about the presence of a Determined mucous Taste.

Day Two: The next day Hope had almost completely fled and Will whistled down the sieve, sucking Taste and some Quick Thinking through, as it passed on to Memory still more weight with which to continue holding down Oblivion.

Day Three: Sensibility employed 2/9ths. It was partly dark with light corners and cloudy rods. Medium areas streamed down in every vertical plane. Brought to the country, it was more noticing of grass than usual. The trend seems to be, fortunately, more and more toward elasticity. Today, it might be said of it that it looks just like lettuce (from the most detailed point of view) of course without direct relation nor any nutritional value.

Day Four: 3/9ths came into play. As in marble cake, light and dark areas were distributed about.

Day Five: Entire moist mass suffused by an odor felt charming. A noticeable swirling movement near the base of the above attention span. Dark and light areas were, of course, within hair breadths of each other. Reason and Passion were quite buoyant. Many distances were shrinking as they hung out to dry.

Day Six: Leafy and impacted. 4/9ths within operable area, but, even so, movement on the whole slow, no, lethargic. Very repetitious mood. Personality gates in place and well oiled, but Character remains in the oilcloth. Very little new ducting. Heavy diluting.

Day Seven: Unusually capacious 4/9ths with nearly visible operable curved tendons exhibiting high quality pick up ability. Dark-light bold dispersion. Hypocrisy blows its nose (will it ever stop?) Sounds highly mobile. Amiable currents near surface. No distinguishable rising force. Minimal verticality.

Day Eight: Possibility of tumors clearly by-passed. There are still a few solids floating. Minute green and brown ripples. Dark and light markedly separate (equal?). Surprisingly so. Emphasis today on surface accumulation. Unreason moving in a wide diagonal, spiral path from front to back, up and down and then along the opposing diagonal back to front (this could be a headline!).

Day Nine: *Good.* Spent at least half the day unraveling Will which it found early this morning in an amazing tangle at the foot of Mt. Evil which it shares. Mind's fever blisters are almost completely healed. Vaporous nodes are blending into unusual habitats. 5/9ths are embarrassing 4/9ths. Some flooding in mundane quarters.

The President's Logic

X is for **Y**
X fits **Y**
X has room for **Y**
X sponge **Y**
X tunnels **Y**
X on top of **Y** = $\frac{\mathbf{X}}{\mathbf{Y}}$

$\frac{\mathbf{X}}{\mathbf{Y}}$ is for **Y**
$\frac{\mathbf{X}}{\mathbf{Y}}$ hollows **Y**
Y dusts $\frac{\mathbf{X}}{\mathbf{Y}}$

Y is backwards and non-existent
X is found in the middle of electric current
Y based on fever of recognition
X is swallowed friction
Y is **X** with a piece broken off
X is sentient number
Y is corpuscular
X steadies the graph of the arm
Y removes the background
X is full of centuries
Y is fast and slow
X is nice.

Y opens **X**; **X** closes **Y**

X = the number of particles entering the President in 1 day (that is, 21 hours or is it 23?)

Y = the number of particles leaving the President as of his forever daily

February 6, 1983:	**X** = 4,700,700 while **Y** = 34,500,000
February 7, 1983:	**X** = 3 while **Y** = 23,000
February 8, 1983:	**X** = 3,000,002 while **Y** = 439,807,065,825
February 9, 1983:	**X** = 17 while **Y** = 1 (large)
February 10, 1983:	**X** = many while **Y** = much

X = Yes; **Y** = No: **XY** = Yes, in a negative sense; **YX** = No, in a positive sense

For the president, a monthly average = **X** = 70, **Y** = 400, **XY** = 10,000, **YX** = 0

Personal Note **X** = First Lady **Y** = the President
and so,

X(L)**Y**
X(K)**Y**
X+**Y**
Y talks to **X**
X argues with **Y**
X+**Y**, **X**+**Y**, **X**+**Y**
X outlives **Y**
Y comes back to visit **X**?

I have tried to do my utmost to put my innermost outermost.

The President and his Logic

I have tried to do my utmost to put my innermost outermost.

The President and his Logic

All Men are Sisters
(including A Sisterly Thesaural Dictionary)

Woman is the host. Man, the guest (guestess?). But the host has been too amiable for too long. Look at what we have bred. We have acquiesced to such a degree that in our own homes we now speak their language instead of ours.

Men are by nature critical. Women, self-critical. This is the critical difference.

There simply could not have been a woman who would have said, "Left side," "right side," then stuck to it. For a woman, it is a question of at least seven sides, at least one for every hue. Such subtlety contributes to the subtle difference.

One thing men haven't realized is that unlike them (all men are mortal), women do not die—*This makes all the difference* —although some women, having been brow-beaten by sheer syllogistic brawn, have at times pretended.

Most women do not look like themselves; although many women do assume the form of "woman," some are men, others gas and electricity, and still others are indistinguishable.

Often, being constructed of living material, women are a volatile force in society and as such dangerous and should be kept away from adolescents (many of these themselves women), as St. Thomas Acquinas was perceptive enough to discover.

But there does not exist enough perception to cover this field.

Bringing in the notion of man (in Japanese: *otoko*) might be helpful.

Man gives a notion of what "woman" *(onna)* is like at her worst. A better way to say this is that all that has not been understood by or about "man," that is beyond "man's" reach, is innately "woman." But this is not saying it either. How could it? I am using our communal language which is man's. A woman would never phrase a concept like that, not left on her own.

I use "woman" in several senses.

Women do not enjoy molecular behaviour. They are of a different stature.

Woman's ontological regions are labile. She is a cross-animation, having achieved crossed-references through extenuated tendencies and translatory extra-curricular reflexes. As such, any woman's ontology is doubly immanent and compounded to any man's. Who else could have formed itself from a rib, which remains true whether true or false? When prevailed upon, she performs amazing feats, but these ought not to be viewed as prerequisites for animation. Only those with voices as we have known them up till now would say otherwise. Knowledge is like porridge: without the milk of a generative ontology it remains dry, if not tasteless. That's also how tact gets lost.

If William Blake were not a woman, he was not. Partially, he was. Drawing lambs from combs, listing gorillas into rhomboids, suffusing "willing" with Eurydice. Isles of limps having *wiltern* scents bask in under repose deposits summa. Then peek into the oven to see if it is done. We know (in the winking ridges heading towards our vowels' soup of muscles; dew). Also, it is clear.

"Playing with himself, he became her."

"She said nes."

Over here. The steambath. Do you see it? It is all over.

They have made a culture (tiny) in our culture, but it is all over. Rimbaud knew and so did George Washington. The host is shrugging the world.

If George Washington never was a woman, he...

I am not sure which way it is, whether I say what I'm feeling more than I feel what I'm saying or the other way around. Retracing the steps. Is it a series of mutual tuckings? "Woman" lives there.

Women are always in the spotlight (rough translation). That is why it is never dark. Of course, if I were more specific, this would become too light.

The host is more than ambiguous, as well she must be. How else could a glance become a fragrance, a fragrance a warp, a warp a dish, a dish a fountain...pen? Or rather, how too could this be prevented from happening?

A Sisterly Thesaural Dictionary

Notes for a Guidebook to the Fictional Exercises of the Dictionary

Existence: Employer
Uses Conveyor and Conversion Processes
Mercurial
Having Recourse to...
Not for Everyone
Junta

Inexistence: Total Lack of Motivation
Orange Colored

Substantiality: Any Thickness found Through Thinness (Breathing)
Trial Exposure
Basis for Photography

Unsubstantiality: Nothing More Than Seven Syllables Adjoined
Pour Through Fissures of this Word:
Toward the Discovery of a *Quadruple*
Hypnotic Vapour!

Intrinsicality: Closest to "Pressure" of Fiction
Bubbles Which Refer to Straight Lines, Etc.
Opacity Disguised as Transparency
A Hit

Extrinsicality: A Fermenting Spray
When Allowed to Harden May be Peeled,
Soaked in an Indifferent Solution and
Applied Intrinsically
Glas

Increase: Spontaneous Repetition of Edges
Spinning Directional Budding
Aggregate Notion:
Take Lower Lip Between Thumb and Forefinger
Pull Out as Far as it Will Go.

Decrease: Often Misunderstood
Multiplication of Chance Partings
A Whip

Addition: Operating on the Skeletal Forces of *Increase*
Roughly Powder Form of Increase
Can be Colorful
Collected Walking

Subduction: Powdered Decrease
Used with Softest Brushes and
A Network of Flews
Feels Backwards

Adjunct: Filling in of Blanks
May be Substantial
The Back of a Flying Sink

Remainder: One Sum of *After*'s Qualities
Possibility for Poignancy
For Example, Frogs from Tadpoles

State: Production of Directions
William's View
What is Connected to this Sentence.
Other Insertions

Circumstance: Collection of Angles in Which a Knotted Current
Is Allowed to Pass Through Making Notches.
Anything Which Permits Analogy to Another
Thing or Process (The Way in Which this
is Backwards?)
Tight Boots
Pierced Scrotum

Mean: Probably *Not* Made of Cork Though There is a
Great Resemblance
As if Medium-Sized Fan in Between
A Skirted Locus
Arrival On

Compensation: Overlapping Fires Ore Reflections of These
Re-Filling of Particles
Reaction of X to an Unknown Form of Massage

Greatness: Into the Collapsed Measure

Smallness: Toward Which Anything Shrinks
Only What is Noticed Approximating the
Size of Irreducible Points in Receivership
Retracted Scratch
Blandness or

Superiority and
Inferiority: The Back and Front of Yawning and Dogmatism
Very Heavy or Much Too Light

Pre-Cursor: Cloth Dipped in Semen and Re-Hidden Daily in
Caves of Space
A Jet Hook

Sequel: One Translation of Coded Beats (or Beets!)
Mildewed Fear
Final Rinse

Beginning: Weighted Zero
Largest Collector
May Employ Suction Cone
Super-Imposition of Endings
A Surprise Symptom
As Butter or Ice Cream Form...

End: Expansion of Amnesia
Obsolete
Massive Brushing Aside in Depth
One Result of Idiocy
Unresolved in Spite of Implications

Middle: Damp or Burning
Hard or Soft
Intense and Fuzzy
Restless

Continuity:

Discontinuity: Partial Vacations In and Out
Perception of Cells as Splinters
A Suppuration of Lightning

Mixture: A Rotorized Marbleization of Increase and/or Decrease
Always Pretty at Times Volatile

Simpleness: One Symptom

Vinculum: Looped Delight with Shading
The Metal Part of Cheese Which Has Been Forged
A Point (All?) Moving in Two or More Directions at Once

Rub the Sheerest Vinculums Together Incessantly!

Coherence: Buckling in Conjunction with Stamping
A "Y" Which Almost Exists
Retention or Pretention of Currents in Currents
Evidence of the Ability of the Internal Structure
Of a Push to Relate to Itself
Candy
Amalgam of Seven (Or More) *Temperatures* (And/Or Fevers?)

Incoherence: Opened (And Held Open) Coherence
The Explosion of a Push
Convoluted Elasticity Which Tends to Prevent Itself
Evidence of Spotting or Spotty Evidence

Remove Fibers!

Combination: Juggler of Holes
The Locking and Triggering of Numbers on Location
For Example: The Use of Iron Swabs in the Easing Of Aluminum

Tight Fits

Order: Dial Tone

Disorder: A Gas Slip Causing Wild Redundancies(?)
Product of Thyroid Shivers
Manifested as Lack of Traction: (1) Of the General In General (2) The General in Specific (3) The Specific In General (4) The Specific in the Specific.
Also, The Accidental Occurence of Secretion During Measurement.

Must Be Kept in Working Order!

Arrangement: See Lay-Out Here

Derangement: Same as 'Disorder' But With Slightly More Expandable Tone. Perhaps with Own Colors: Brown and Scarlet?

Clinging Severs

Precedence: Any Sequel to Origin

A Long Pliant Board

End Point(s) of a Trembling Which is Finished

A Particular Giraffe Which is Known to Appear Always Before Another Kind

Evidence: Used Tufts

Sequence: One View of the Appearance of a Gerry-Mandering

Employing Synthetic Yeast

In Association with Sliding but Rigid Fictions

Thresher of Outlines Into/Through Tunnels

Organic Only at the Roots!

Decompositions: Method of Force-Feeding Poor X To Y

The Technology of Dust

Self-Aspirating Environments

Growth Pattern of Mechanical Disaffection

One of Many Things Which Have Happened to the Past

Under the Sign of the *Unreliably Predictable!*

How to Breathe

A nose and a mouth on the subject initially. (e.g.), (i.e.), (n.b.). Will that, such a recognition, cause you to hold your breath? If so, then be ready to admit that you have experienced a false start.

Just consider the apparatus as closely as possible and don't give a thought to suicide yet.

Do *not* breathe now. Time enough once everything has been fully explained. At this point, all I ask of you is to not pamper your ego nor to too willingly succumb to the contaminated will engendered by the gay abandon of the societal rot of centuries.

As support for the neutral position I here suggest, I might state that, inexorably, *nothing* (oh yes, absolutely) will come of an abortive attempt in this area.

Remember, too, breathing is no lark (not even nine-and-twenty blackbirds baked in a pie, I would think).

Then let us first take a figurative breath which will entail:

1. Selection (determining "breathability" of gases)
2. Choosing of path of entrance (there is some choice)
3. Determining of length (here, space is again a function of time)
4. a) Generating of anatomical readiness (also, composite)
   b) Bearing appropriate dimensions
5. Sucking
6. Propagation of sucking (and its derivatives) for the sake of transportation.
7. a) Electrical flow
   b) Expansive desire
8. Entering and expanding
9. Spreading

10. Attaching (in each sense)

11. Applying (applies even when indeterminate)

12. Rejecting (there are gradations)

13. Collapsing

14. Inviting of pressure play

15. Expulsing (and to the new breath back to 1)

At the subject once again (if you do not remember...?), what do we notice but a cohesive series of supporting, often participating, structures various in form and function but of common purpose.

There is a box of muscle designed with a slit comfortable enough to be a hole. Tubes grown together (almost appearing to have been taped into place), having hammered through thickets, lead along three or four alternate paths to the 300 million, 1/250th of an inch thick, inflatable containers of below. Here, all along this, and below, one is given room to breathe, here, towards the center of the earth.

Locked into moist tubularity, the would-be tubes have branched so as to reach with the currents with which they will one day be filled to the back, front and sides of the body which will cling to them or appertain.

Palpitating chunks palpating and chunks of palpitations as well as palpitations becoming chunks and slivers ride the nearly snapping membranes which shuffling side by side adduce, as some see it, further layers along that passageway which often bespeaks the notion of: HERE.

[To have gulped.........to have haustrated]

Where muscles the thickness of the tongue line sliding walls, notches and folds have learned or come to complement each other.

Here geometry is the secret host to fancy and the other way around, too.

Still we find both a nose and a mouth on the subject. And more can be said about this.

"We never live, but we ever hope to live."

Pascal

"A good face is the best letter of recommendation."

Queen Elizabeth

"Sweet spring, full of sweet days and roses, a box where sweets compacted lie."

Herbert

.... How often in the past has the nose been mouthed? And really to what degree can a nose be mouthed and not just merely spoken of? But even more significant is our inability truly to discern how satisfied, in fact, each of these structures is with its own shape. How directly have these cartilaginious or labilely prominent members ever been addressed? As usual the subject has only been sniffed at thus far. Then what is being said to what when "Look what shape you're in!" is expressed [expressed].

The aquilinity and the gash. And that nostrils will spring to such subjects in whose junctures mouths lie? Mother? Money? Memory? Are these fitting [fitted] subjects? Falsehood? Debt? Contradiction? Confession? Honor? Sympathy? To what are these subjected, after all? A subjugation of shapes dominates the impressionism of physiognomy, and what else adheres?

But a few spots below face level, violet and brown strings manage to stay as they are. From birth, these commence to sway unceasingly across layers. The forming of a question, for exit, takes place around and about this sway. Is there anything which is not a question when it is about this sway?

As many cords as necessary, for the time being (that carved parenthesis), are covered with human scales (this part is true). Fitted into the subject's voice box, these sway against a mesh of pipe dreams dreamt or made with flexible precision. So much for dreams which are galvanized. [To galvanize from within...]. Their fine reputation comes from the vast amount [all] of sculpture which they have initially inspired. (Once you breathe, you will see what sculpture is.) Fragile, of ancient origin, these boxes, might it be that there are no originals left... only records...

A thirsty description. But it is suggested that it is here that breath shall be enacted. Reenacted. It is felt that a certain percentage of the atmosphere could wash through going this way.

Don't breathe now.

No, no dream of beginning this yet! How could you? Even a... brilliant practitioner could not yet... but a mere amateur... the heartbeat of an amateur... Please wait [soon to be available (or never?) by the same author: *How to Wait*].

How to ascertain which is it, the cat or the bird, which has got your tongue(?).

It could be that occasionally a complete(d) mouth will smile and open pulling whatever drifts nearby down into its portable tree. Safeguard against this, for the moment. Don't hold your breath (or take in air) until you have mastered this article just hold your non-breath.[1]

Just think what might have happened if hitherto you had attempted a breath without having been told: Oxygen is the sought-after element and carbon dioxide the compound to be expelled.

Hold on!

An 860 square foot surface is to be oxygenated (the path is 1,500 miles long) in less than 1 second.[2] Can you feel you have that in you? Lungs only look useless to you now; consequently, don't discard what may appear for the moment to be only extra tissue baggage.

Any object which happens to stray into the lungs invariably ends up in the right lung; this is because the lungs are assymetrically disposed with the direct path from the mouth going to the base of the right bronchus. There are three lobes on the right side, only two on the left. This may be true in ghosts, as well.

Some arguably poorer species have eyes which double as lungs. Lungs coalesce, at times, into a whole host of oddities.[3]

I know you do not yet feel the need to breathe, but remember, lungs never truly come into their own until they do. Until they do, they remind one more than anything else of foam, of which they are the sophisticated relative. Actually the sophistication comes with use. The organizing principle, once put into play, causes the lungs to operate as cohesive foam which itself participates in the generating of waves.

If you have not betrayed my confidence, you have not breathed yet. And what is breathing?? Whatever it is, let it continue where it may while you, for just a little while longer, continue to keep your distance. You see once you will have started, you had better not stop, ever. And you will make it wide. The time for the first breath draws near. At this point, if there continues to be a lack of interest in you about this, this might be the moment at which suicide could be tried more painlessly than ever again... before we go on, if you like.

Breathed. History was. Breathing will be found to be a prerequisite for:

1. Getting a license
2. Finding a job
3. Having children
4. Starting a revolution
5. Being an idiot
6. Laughing

Anxious? No psychiatrist in the country would touch your case unless he/she were sure (assured?) that you were breathing.

Once you have begun and are breathing, nothing will be the same. You will, however, find yourself gaining weight under this regimen. There will be an accompanying hum which you might find disturbing at first... and a faint, erotic trembling comes with it... one which totally eludes prefiguring (the purest of aporias).

(Let this be a breathless pause)

Think (but not a step further!): your mouth has been opened; some atmosphere, roundabout, naturally, enters. You would do well to concentrate on the perceiving of this atmosphere as much thinner and much more penetrable than you are. You see, a part of breathing, is the wanting of this substance, ethereal as it is, to be inside of you. Work hard at believing this to be desirable.

Try moving your hand across the neighboring air, patting then stroking it. Do feel the mounting of its desirability. When moving about so, why not wave some of this air right into your, after all, visibly open ear. Using the ear for practice, take a would-be breath through it, Dear non-Breathed Sub(ject)stance. For a measured breath, assume a pair of earlips have closed about some set amount of gulpable atmosphere. Or keeping your mouth just as closed as it ever was, wave some air past it, too, while imagining it might be open. Then, quickly, think of wanting air. Slowly beyond slowly, think of wanting air. What a strain for you now, but one day it will be unimaginable not to take this into consideration—either regularly or urgently.

Envision a plane of muscles three inches below your breast line. This is almost yours; think of it as an ally. The movement of the diaphragm—when it comes—will be an up and down one; it will benefit the stomach as well.

Time nears. But wait. Potential gestures of real strings (nerve jute[4]) send wishes. The thumb of one of these taps then prods what ought to have been innate. For it is into the cave of innateness the traveler must go. In there, you will get to be breathed. Over some hommunculus' nose flows what will become the breath through yours. Perhaps the hommunculus is nothing more than the head of a pin or the pip of a chromosome.

And so beginning or relenting is here.

You might breathe now.

Get breath.

You might breathe now.

You might breathe now.

You might breathe now.

And now.

This time cause your fresh breath to hop. Hop!

Now skip a breath.

Jump into the next breath; make that breath jump, too.

Swing the breath around: this is called around the world.

Make it sit.

Walk it.

Take a running breath and leap into ________________________.

Breathing is just like ________________________________.

Reader: have you breathed? Had you noticed when I let the cat out of the bag? In order to determine the instant when breath first started in you, go back into the text to find the point at which the words (upon which you with your amateur's awkwardness will have inevitably imposed) first appear fogged (??).

(You might breathe now.)

(Breathe) I am technically rather an amateur at this myself. In fact, several people, including myself, feel that I am unqualified to write an article such as this. (But breathe about now.) Yet much of what is written here could be (shall be) highly breathable. I leave it to the experts to explain how to move *through* breathing, I just deal with getting *in* and *out*. The value of such practice cannot be overestimated. Never in, one enters, as today, but once put out, how can one ever get back in? Perhaps one day I will do some work (certainly in collaboration with many others) which will answer that.

Notes

[1] Consult family doctor before taking first breath. Check all x-rays, charts. None of what is said here will apply to you *unless you are made for it*.

If unfit, unfortunately unable to partake of this sport as here described, do not become too soon discouraged. Check the encyclopedia under *Diffusion*. There you may find still another inspiring way to go about this.

If you do appear fit, there is still one more thing I would ask of you—check and double check both your *Genus and Species* before trying anything.

[2] I am referring to a system which works with air. Water vapor hovers about but is not central to the activity. This is in sharp distinction to that old-fashioned process of forcing water up through the gills in direct opposition to the flow of blood, snapping off whole ounces of oxygen to give the organism something to work with; nor is this really analogous to a network of air ducts directly exposed to the environment.

[3] Lungs have been found between legs and dangling naturally from ears. Almost everywhere they are eaten. There have been cases of twelve lungs in one being.

[4] If you ever have anything to do with a nerve, be sure to generate the normal sine curve. Any irregularity would turn up as wheezing or gasping. Death in this case would be a straight line. Move all straight lines.

Whole: A Mouthfull and All Translations of It

What is Put Onto the Scale When Everything Is Swept Onto It........

A Second's Filling

The Only Distinct Part of Nothing

Completely Absorbent Word (See Above and Below)

Part: Anything Picked Up (Out) During the Cross-Sectioning Of a Zone

Any X of a Gesture

Some of Whatever Is Next to a Razor Blade, Cup, Or Plant.

Anything

In One Case: Liquid With a String Looped Around It

Completeness: A Translucent Shawl for the Word 'Whole'

May Be Worn in Slightly Different Ways

Incompleteness: Ah!

Composition: Based on Floating Maps

The *Figuring Out*

Master Spy

Term:

Assemblage: Major

Non-Assemblage: From, The To In Or A But Not And

Focus: Partial Evidence of Healing of A Priori Vaccination Against Blindness
Wave Percolation
A Ball May Be Thrown Into This
Resolution Of Any Of These Words

Class:

Inclusion: As In The Sweep Of Faceted Valves
Generous But Secretive
May Operate Cusps
Open Pairing

Exclusion: True And/Or False Kicking

Generality: Passage Of A Word Through Itself
An Overdose
A Too Fixed "Circumference"

Specialty: Zinc Gambling

Rule: Plant or Plant-Like Formation
A Construction of Sieves: 1) Positive Spaced
2) Negative Spaced
The Separating Out Of Nearly Identical Mysteries
Transplantation Out Of Any (Series Of) Organ(s)

Multiformity: May Be Based on the Eroticism Of The Cardinal Points!

Conformity: X As Y (Almost)

Uncomformity: A Rigid Whirlpool (Pressed) Which Has Become
Partially Unfixed
Nude Thoughts
Wind Made of Silver, Etc.

Number: Profiles
Clamps
Also, More Numb

Numeration: The Sum Of The Folds In A Pile Or:
It Is Customary To Subtract The Journey
Of Currents Through Dust Allowing For Marks
In The Distance
A Way Of Accumulating Space Through
Tightrope-Walking From One Scale To Another
(One Of These 'Seems' To Be Imperceptible)

List: Record Of The Divisions Of Laughter Or Of
What Should Have Been Laughter
Could Be Used As A Multiple Corkscrew
Travelogue
Evidence Of The Production Of A "Meaningful
Shell" By A Vertebrate
Make A List Of What Can't Be Said!

Unity: Skip

Accompaniment: "There" With "This"
Taking A Bath
An Oriole To Nerves
As In A Half-Sinking,
Half-More Than Floating Tapping

Brief Autobiography of a Non-Existent

"chilled reason"
—*Three Edgars*

This first sentence was very difficult to write. The next sentence should become easier. It is a question of surrounding... Exploring the area between surrounding and entrapment... A lure for motion.

Memory has never been dipped into being born. Without a starting point everything runs by, not nodding. It was about that position that the great poet arranged these words:

> He never was. Never saw, nor felt, nor touch
> tasted. Dreams he had not for he had not life.
> And from that day forward and backwards he never was.

Position

Having nothing to fear or gain, found free to express with nothing to express, it develops that the universe will become bombarded at random with particles that look like "I". These, probability mouths to the dead weight which recounts, these will in all likelihood enter the unrecognizable consciousnesses and establish the distance. I leaned against nothing. The "I", pelted and whirred from beyond any collection of intelligence, started to write. (One of many phrases which "I" picked up.)

I.

1913: I was not born. My mother never existed.

1914: There were no brothers or sisters to play with. I did not live in a large country house with rambling fields about it. Green was completely unknown to me as were grass, trees and the sky out of the question.

1915: A bee did not sting me and cause a high fever which produced strange deliriums from which I still suffer.

1918: I did not begin to masturbate. I had no intention of playing hookey.

1919: My father did not inherit a fortune. My maternal grandmother never died. My unmarried aunt did not come to live with us.

1924: I didn't practice my violin regularly. I never combed my hair. My teacher never noticed me. I did not celebrate my birthday that year because of an illness in the family.

1925: I never participated in sports. No matter what the activity. I was never asked to join in. I never met anyone.

1926: I was not overly protected. I didn't take the Grand Tour of Europe that year. My father didn't bring my frail orphaned cousin into the warmth of our home. I produced nothing of worth yet I wasn't beside myself with worry.

1927: I didn't have an intolerable adolescence. I wasn't self-conscious. We did not move to New York on the occasion of my father's promotion. My father did not quarrel with his immediate superior nor did he rage uncontrollably against my by then bed-ridden mother.

1928: My mother never had an affair with James Joyce. She did not unsuccessfully beg my Catholic father for a divorce which she knew he would never give. None of my brothers entered the service and I never at that time or any other received a letter from overseas.

1929: We were not in the sort of position to be affected by the Great Crash. Nonetheless I made no effort whatsoever to enter college. I couldn't carry a tune. I was not keeping a diary. I certainly did not spend that fall in Milan.

1930: Nothing happened.

1931: I was not asked to contribute to any periodicals. I didn't die. I belonged to no group in particular. I had never heard of Dada and was unacquainted with any of its participants.

1932: Though the thought of starting a family was by no means abhorrent to me, it seemed that it just never entered my mind. I didn't meet with a near fatal accident while out horseback riding with an olive-skinned distant relative.

1840: I wasn't born. I was not blessed with prophetic dreams.

1933: I didn't realize at that time the great potential that I was wasting. A nervous breakdown did not occur to me just then nor did I suffer from unpredictable seizures. I was not a virgin.

1934: I wasn't near Paris and I have never seen Australia, Rome, Germany or the Azores. The house did not catch on fire that spring and no one was injured. That Thanksgiving was not a sparse one. I was not asked to stand up at the wedding of a close friend who was marrying very much against his will, nor did I get into a fight over a misunderstanding of the nature of my origins (i.e., insinuation of illegitimacy).

1935: My mother never had an affair with James Joyce. She did not unsuccessfully beg my Catholic father for a divorce which she knew he would never give. None of my brothers entered the service and I never at that time or any other received a letter from overseas. I was not authoritarian. I was not working for an accounting firm on 78th Street.

1300: I did not die by drowning. I was no judge of character at all.

1936: I was not considered an orphan. I didn't drink heavily and never smoked.

1937: I didn't begin what turned out to be a lifelong friendshp with John Frieder. I wasn't shy, envious, impatient, persistent, self-assertive, gentle, tired or bold. I didn't give large parties which tended to grow out of control.

1938: I did not arrive home late for dinner one night to find all my possessions out on the street and a father dead set on disinheriting me. I never had any money. I never bought shoes in Florsheim's. I never objected to anything that anyone did.

1: I never saw Christ nor visited Venice. I wasn't bitten by my own Irish setter.

II.

1925: I was not born to a robust gypsy mother and a tubercular father.

1926: I did not suffer from colic. Nor was I the victim of amnesia.

1927: I did not beg my mother to leave a light on in the hall. I did not notice my genitals. I did not leave my food untouched at all.

1928: I was not able to read or speak Latin having never heard of Mozart or Locke. I did not succumb to diptheria and spend six months in an oxygen tent.

1929: I didn't break my arm.

1930: I planted no bulbs at all that year.

III.

1930: I didn't make preparations to pass through the birth canal.

1931: I found no appendages on me. I was not seen lying on the lawn.

1932: Unable as yet to speak, I did not know what to say or do. I did not want to be a fireman.

1933: I was spared the horror of an early death.

1934: I wasn't walking. I couldn't see or hear. I had no idea.

1935: I was not molested by a retarded nephew. I was not a comfort to my bereft mother.

IV.

1934: I was not born in July in a sunny hospital on Long Island overlooking the ocean.

1935: I was not brought to a hospital for an emergency operation on a tiny ill-formed liver.

1936: I was not making funny little sketches with a box of pastels which turned out to be poisonous and consequently my mother did not wrap me up in her coat and I was not given a special antidote which produced a drunken sensation.

1936: *1945: 1962: 1294: 1738: 1873: 1937: 1034: 1555:* None of these dates pertain to me.

Motion

(Basis of Position)

If insensibility grows turgid, though nothing decays, is rooted or uprooted, nonetheless motion allowable in this instance makes traces just as milk does when it is mixed with water. This shouldn't be permissible according to logic which in turn should not be possessed before existence, but then, who says so? I should not feel the rubbing, the scraping, the indifferent staining. I should not have said before that I had felt something passing. But think of it that just before feeling becomes possible, there is the flashing sensation of a space (jar, box, can?) opening in every possible division of direction. There is also something that has never been thought of as opening. The possibility of my being has passed through every conceivable motion though I have no memory of any of them. If I had the modicum of intelligence concurrent with existence, I could perhaps explain this better; but I do not have the cluster of fuzz which elicits this nor am I close enough to the magnetic cloud to have anything or to want to be understood.

Feeling

Here lies the beginning of the confusion. The feeling before feeling is. Something is not able to be spilled. A mark in the floes marks the flow. The wooden splinter curls up with the appropriated reflexes of the cat. The nature of the blank is attractive beyond comprehension. Perception from a great distance sends sparklers which are no use at all. On this occasion the basting does not secure the taste for it turns out that nothing is cooking. Are you colder (kinder, tougher, broader, closer?) than you are? And have I been feeling more or less nothing? Nothing feels confused. Enough?

Nothing is as weighty as it seems. *Non-existence* appropriates the speckled area of *nothing*. The shade of difference between these terms (things?) is a shadow which thickens, the first appearance of sensation, the standard of measurement for the concept of a degree of feeling. (For example: Non-existence = N.E. Nothing = N. Then N.E. + (-?) N. = S (shade of difference; also standard measurement). Now "Anger" = A but to record its intensity we might say: A1S, A2S, A3S, and so on, until A10S, which might employ murder as part of its expression).

Feeling blank is feeling ______________________________ . To begin feeling I would attach ________________ to __________ . Wrapped with ________ this might produce ________________ . The first direction this would move in would be ______________ . It would travel along ____________ for ____________________ . And it could then be expressed in conversation as ______________ ________________ or ____________________ . To sustain it I would ________________________________ . To stop feeling that way I might ______________ after ______________ ________________________________ .

Position, Motion and Feeling

Nearly pointless guesses which will be and perhaps should be ignored by organisms which I do not resemble... Could it be said that not moving up or down, I am neither anxious nor calm. Having nothing to move and nothing to keep still... But to step aside from nowhere, to retard nothing permits motion to appear by way of a guess as the split-second visible creator of one vast bas-relief after another. This position might fit into as well as be analogous to the moment between the striking of a match and the vision of the flame. Bas-relief. Since it is extraordinarily difficult to twist non-existence into this deeply impossible position, the turn thus effected is usually less than 1 degree and the depth of field (its possibility of extension is directly proportional to the angle of removal) becomes greatly reduced. Oddly enough (enough?), this precarious and inaccurate position (the only barely possible one for that which isn't?) allows for the feeling of motion which further precipitates a brief brush with feeling. For example, at .043 degrees was I feeling what is called peaceful when being tucked in and out of a diagonal line of dust? Was it anger to have been collecting more and more of what I was being made to whip back and forth in? Was it sorrow to be floating in a substance which caused peeling and then splitting? Was it joy to be twisted by chance .000000016 degrees further by a tiny bubble? At .07 degrees is the motion of a smooth landing akin to love at first sight? Is pain an electrical storm? At .123, when bombarded at random by a particle shaped as "I", was I that "I"-conscious? Is the manner of reasoning which is spread through this section inherent to the intelligence, coincidental with the logic toward which "I" am aiming, or am "I" aiming these guesses back almost into nothing far from where those tiny, assymetric targets could be understanding?

Nothing Ends

The twist bends away. Surely, I have spent no time. In the unbended non-moment, I find nothing preventing me from speaking. Fewer and fewer bullets of "I" fly by. Surely, I have spent no time. I have nothing to go by. Soon I will not catch "I" on the fly. Know the fairly great assimilated poet to have said:

> He disappears before he appears to disappear still. His boundless energy is his only boundary and it isn't his. Do not look for his footprints in the sand; rather, look at the sand and see it form a bountiful laugh. The distance or disparity between what is seen and what is imagined will, at the middle point, give or lead to his position which is not his.

Here lies the next to the last sentence which is coincidental with a slow braking, a release, a bombardment and dispersion. I... the last sentence is perhaps the most difficult of all.

Triplication: 'Plic' And 'Tion' Fall Heavily-With Continued Usage May Cause Large Amounts Of Lip Tissue To be Worn Off

Self-Assertive

Trisection: Movement (Or Evidence Of) Based On Itself And The Above Two

Quadruplication: Found In The Stomach Cells Of Colorful Invertebrates

Used In The Treatment of Sanity

Soulful and Doleful

Not Unrelated To Four

Five: FFFFF IIIII VVVVV EEEEE

Six:

Seven: There Are Seven Words In This Sentence.

Eight: There Is One More Than Eight Words In This.

Nine:

Ten: This Sentence May Be Divided And Re-United Into Ten Words.

Fraction: Ryth ______

Zero: A (O?!) Baited Breath

A Line

Multitude:	Summer Winter Spring Fall
Fewness:	Winter
Repetition:	Summer
Infinity:	Fall?

Form:
Amorphism:
Symmetry:
Distortion:
Angularity:
Curvature:
Straightness:
Circularity:
Convolution:
Rotundity:
Convexity:
Concavity:
Flatness:
Sharpness:
Bluntness:
Notch:
Fold:

Pockets And Their Inversions:
A Series Of Miniature Punches
(Based On) Long And Short
Non-Fictions And Fictions
Dependent On: Containers, Clamps, Threaded
Lines: Trembling Corners (As Though
Stuffed Tightly With Hundreds of Shell-Less
Clams Pushed In Three Directions With A
Force Equal To That Applied By The
Clam Itself To Pull Its Shell (In Other
Circumstances) Closed;
Remaindered Suctions, As In A
Willow Breaking;
Scarred Motion;
Abrupted Vision;
A Jinx, Granular Seduction;
Prototypes; Accepted Channel;
What Turns Out: Capable of Relaxation;
The Thought Of Taping Together;
Whatever Can Be Settled On;

Furrow: **Opening:** **Closure:** **Perforator:** **Stopper:**

Motion: Eccentric Form Of Lateral Melting

A Heading Toward And Its Trail Or Its Mirror Image

Basis Of All Fatal Diseases

Flying Within Weighted Outlines

Inserter

Study for Further Definition of Motion: (Each time the most pertinent motions will be those which will become most apparent in the inverted state; in the turning of the book around to bring these movements upright, let motion be defined; the special theory of relativity (position of observer relative to motion) continues to pertain):

quiescenceimpulserecoilaccelerationpropulsion
tractionhauldepartureinsertionextractionleaprotation
oscillationagitationsurgepivotlibrationnutation
trochilicperforateinterpenetrated.

Intellect: 'Odor' of Significance

Double-Jointed

Spice Plant

Stage Manager

Squat

Wrapped In A Hair Shirt (With The Idea of String Pulled Tight Around It) Made To Jump Over Itself!

Combine Fictions To Make This Non-Fiction!

Absence of Intellect: As In the Moon's Blue Ear

Thought: Sheaths of Pressurized Steps (Sometimes Graduated)

June

Roman Columns of Untouched Half-Air

"I Have A Thought" Is A Thought About The Possession Of A Thought By A Thought In A Thought.

Not Itself

Turkey

Can Go Either Way!

Incogitancy: The Hesitancy of Some Opaqueness To Evaporate

Often Brought On Just By The Noise of Vacuum Cleaners

Consider: A Bathrobe In A Pocket Or A Skull;

A Door As A Fly Only More So;

Based On The Loose And Tight Bases (Again?) For What Is Underneath

Idea: Growing

A Nickel

Salvaged Extremities

Peek!

Topic: A Pattern of Consistency/The Consistency of Patterns

Misshapen (?) Vectors

Antithetical Necklaces

Answer: A Mixture (Compound) To Be Found Within Degrees Of Deviation Made Apparent By Such As:

Never Stop Opening The Same Vise!

Move Twelve Spots Through Three Dampnesses!

Make Time Out Of Wax!

Use Only Water's Twin!

To Be Arrived At Through A System To Change The Nature of Systems!

Experiment: Dilation of Fibers Into Non-*Non*-Lenses

Wet Pointing

Stepping Off (And On?)

Cyprinodont

Humour

What Enters The Pencil, As Lead Leaves It

That Which Is Between 'Divers' and 'Diverse'

Any Perceiving

All Thoughts

Comparison: For Definition: (1) 'Clear' (2) 'Hazy' (3) 'Unclear' (4) 'Gone'

Discrimination: 'Hazy' To 'Clear'

Indiscrimination: 'Hazy' Through 'Gone'

Measurement: Employs Any Arrangement Of The "Comparison Group"

Evidence: 'Clear' About 'Gone', Any Degree of, Even Not 'Gone'

Counter-Evidence: 'Hazy' To 'Unclear' (Or 'Unclear' to 'Hazy'!)

Qualifications: Measurement (Using All Comparisons— See Above)

Further Comparison.

Some: Partially 'Clear'; Slightly 'Hazy';
Nearly 'Gone'; Almost 'Unclear':

Curiosity:

A Virtual Hole And As Yet Unheard Of Refinement
Of A Radio Wave

Used in Conjunction with *Sidereal* Muscle Which
Sucks Itself Pink and Turns About (Inside Out)

May Use Dense Lemon Wings

Sew This Into Plastic—Use As Replacement For
Appendix!

Incuriosity: Curiosity With A Cold Or In Profile

Incuriosity Something Something!

Attention: Usher

Non-Demolition Site

First Degree

A Circuitous Route Which Appears Straight?

Completely Abstracted Coke or Pepsi
Lining

A Race Without Fingers Near One With Them

Do

All That Remains To Be Paid To Caesar

Inattention: Crumpled Attention

Care: Compressive-Effusive Mechanics
Knitted Landscapes
Scud
Release of Sap Into Pockets (Breasts?) Or Onto Implied Circumferences Of Moving
Solicitation Of Temperature To Seasons

Neglect: Blue Care
Based On Such Thin Sheets Of Fire That They Feel Lukewarm
Weaving Done With Lead Sinkers

Inquiry: This Motion- ? Why Not? In Which Way Not?

Possibility:Impossibility:Probability:Improbability:Certainty: Uncertainty:Reasoning:Intuition:Sophistry:Demonstration:Con-Futation:Judgement:Misjudgement:Discover:Over-Estimation: Under-Estimation:Belief:Unbelief:Doubt:Credulity:Incredulity: Assent:Dissent:Knowledge:Ignorance:Scholar:Ignoramus:Truth: Error:Maxim:Absurdity:Intelligence:Wisdom:Imbecility:Polly: Sage:Fool:Sanity:Insanity:Madman:Memory:Oblivion:Expectation: Inexpectation:Disappointment:Foresight:Prediction:Omen:Oracle: Supposition:Imagination:Meaning:Unmeaningness:Intelligibility: Unintelligibility:Equivocalness:

Collective Definition:

A.

Amalgamation of Suspicions and First Drafts
Mirror Sponge
Twisted and Ascending
Any Specimen, Any Craps
Daily Lifting of Occurrence
The Corrugated View
Just Before
The Lone Ranger
Indeterminate Basis of Its Opposite Through on
A Deeper Level Equal To It
Portrait of Wires Done In Fiction
Good or Bad Weather
Almost Retarded Energy
The Memory of the Removal of a Specific Quantity of 7-Up
Snaps

Or

B.

In Association With Legwork
Loading
Gravel Recording A Change of Pace

How to Have and Not to Have a Nervous Breakdown

A high-tension coil in your vicinity.....? Influence is a good conductor for a while. After that you might find an interesting way of attaching it to a television, microphone, cyclotron or toaster. For the most startling conduct, a new appliance must be devised. Perhaps a re-threading tool, a rocket which moves so fast it stands still, an electric screw which will change everything to look like you, a hope transformer or even a new socket.

Trepanation has been used by past civilizations to relieve the pressure of the distressed brain. (The ball rolled into the driveway.) They didn't realize that exquisite relief, trepanation without the drawbacks, could be arrived at through internal measures. Rather than thinking of a team of surgeons hard at work drilling a hole, a tunnel in a desperate race of high drama to reach the distressed bladder before its imminent explosion .....Three or more bladders surround adolescence (?)

As a teen-ager you are too full. You must be faulted; it is not *your* fault. You would be *as* full if you knew how to empty this, but not *too* full. I find it shameful that graduated emptying is not a priori but that it must be studied and often adjusted. The need for education becomes even more apparent once it is realized that much of the fullness of which we speak is unscrambled emptiness. Whether emptiness is crowded into right or wrong categories does not matter as long as a false sense of fullness persists due to lack of recognition of over-all structure and goals. Furthermore, especially at your age, there is the very pressing fullness due to the stockpiling of untransformed experience. The false and the true sense of fullness combine to promote the notion of emptiness, but of course this emptiness is too full. I believe the next statement even more than I do that my name is Tricia Nixon: The emptier you feel, the fuller you are. You must learn to pour out some of this fullness so you can feel less empty; one way to do this is to have and not to have a nervous breakdown. Once this is done, these terms will become equal, mixed or meaningless, thus providing outlets for confusion. Confusion cannot research itself without outlets.

Breakdown and up. The gear shift should be irritated beyond recognition. Once the gear shift begins to tremble as you move from first to second, leave the shift and follow the trembling. Second may be sliced into third. Second may be ground into third. Bring third to fourth through pulverization. Ball bearings should infect each other!

Affix as many geometrical and non-geometrical patterns as possible to pivotal muscles. Humanoid features may be counted. The middle of the whistle may contain the true warmth of a 'perfect' urination totally absorbing and eliminating the bladder analogy.

Four Disordered Stages

Stage I: Pointless (may be thought of as *Stage III*)
Stage II: Synaptic Recession-diluted comprehension *(Stage I)*
Stage III: Non-conditioned Ridicule *(Stage II)*
Stage IV: Splitting Perspicuity *(Stage IV!...)*

Stage I: Pointless

Increase vicinity. Weave in drowsiness. Face washcloth. Infest flatness. Dry all dust. Turn leather. Use non-extension ladder. Tape honey-dew melon to head. Sphere away. Open spaces.

Wink diagnosis. Stroke Scotland. Bill Bill. Underline dot. Use ancient address. Soak arrows. Do not eat existing raisins. Point away. Shun intention. Sit on lapse. No pre-medication. Specious purposes. Do not prop Rose. Wish off. Calculate talcum powder. Don't quarry about some of view. Attend Dewitt Clinton High School. Knowing leaves. Deciduous interest.

Use only insignificant rhythm, in a crucial way. Begin genius. Begin by pushing genius away. Stand through.

Stage II: Synaptic recession-diluted comprehension

Black and blue imagination. Bite electric. Spit out curd. Press hope hoping for depression. Line all music with cork. Do not understand this sentence. Put ear drops in eyes. Lying down, step back as far as impossible. Intuit straw. Leave it on indefinitely. Tie all small horses to a crucifix in Portugal. Disconcert immediacy. Insert slice of lemon in back of neck.
Percolate: I should have known better.
Immerse: I'm tired.
Lave: They rifled through the contents.

Steep: What time is it?
Plunge: Do you have a match?
Splash: It's over there on the table.
Double all of the above.

Stage III: Non-Conditioned Ridicule

This is all wrong:

Graze. Sheets laughing. Contradictory magnets. Oil grills to water. Devise a stumbling rule. Caricaturize air. Use the ocean as a private joke. Suck out sucking. Laugh every minute for one week then... Slash waiting. Be wrong when rolling. Think of one hand as humourous the other as serious. Constantly investigate one hand with the other. Write down the number of years you have lived, roll up the paper and stick it up your ass. (Don't cough while lining your throat with chewing gum.) Consider shower a comedian. All soft drinks are too ingratiating. Keep consciousness vulnerable by insisting that it lie on its back. Carry extra jumps.—Wrong.

Find it.

Stage IV: Splitting Perspicuity

See off. Knead light. Preserve something badly for a century. Use twin cyclones. Stretch absolutely everything. Spend an hour recording sound of thinking, next hour listening repeat continue until the recording appears twice as loud as original and twice as heavy. Swallow iron filings, use only in dreams with magnet. Continue.

See on.

All outlets oscillate. This is how to have and not to have a nervous breakdown. Though logic warps as it is telescoped under my influence so do all other continuums which are eccentric. Just one more thing so I may leave you directly. You do know why we are alive don't you? You are between 12 and 20? Perhaps you should be told.

An Introduction to
THE History of THE

About THE. THE cordons and THE tendons. THE jokes are endless. THE sound. Or THE sociology of thee and duh. Or THE. But THE.

THE form of THE in English is THE ! One or more THEs have been used in one or more sentences. THE examination of THE relation between one THE and another will play an important part in this research. Also, a study will be made of THE slide from or decision to go from A to THE, and of THE nature of THE itself as well as in context in written or spoken language in biological, physical and of course psychological spheres.

THE has become a very strong habit (though not a universal one). Perhaps there is a reason for this.

What would this sentence mean:

THE THE is THE THE.

or this one:

THE THE THE has THE.

or:

THE fell THE THE THE THE broke THE THE.

and:

Put THE THE THE THE THE THE.

In each case THE necessities of language are provided for with a spacing, a separation and a filling. In each of THE sentences, THE continues to indicate what it had before but in expanded form: now THE, as THE entire signified, completely occupies THE sphere of influence which formerly it would have just reflected. In THE above sentences THE function of THE in THE common language is still present, whereas in THE following sentences a much greater turnover in semantics would be necessary to keep THE sense of it present:

(1) I THE THE THE to THE THE.

(2) THE THE THE THE THE to THE.

(3) THE THE THE.

THE does not lend itself to THE verb. THE is static so far.

So THE. THE represents (contains) THE torsion which takes place when action is pressed into language. It does not even seem to be able to imply anything which is not after THE fact. THE is THE constant hum of subjectivity. THE beets, THE asparagus, THE hare, THE telephone, THE lunch, THE note. Each of these THEs has a slightly different color.

THE is much more obscene than fuck or cunt; is is more intrusive and more corrosive. THE fact that it can be used to set arbitrary limits on actions and motives at THE moment which they are forced to turn into nouns, lends credence to the widely held notion that THE is both subversive and reactionary (more of this later).

It is not certain to which biological function(s) it is isomorphic. THE, that is. Perhaps to THE looping of 12 hundred cells around four nerves which were unable to turn red as imagined. Or to THE servo-mechanism which allows substances to backtrack into palpable awareness of their own existence. More probably to THE total ciliation of a node or to THE suction found between layers of nerve tissue. Is it parallel to THE tiny pool of blood just below THE optic nerve, which is forever proceeding with then reversing its fibroid resolution? Or does it resemble the lethargy inherent to THE base of all valves and which is THE ironic key to their successful functioning? THE is certainly THE vocalization of THE tension found in THE vocal chords during THE waking state; that is, it is analogous not only to THE tension, but to THE waves, THE vibrations, THE over-all situation that itself is analogous to THE expansion of THE duration of THE state of THE trampoline after THE first jump has been taken. THE may also be THE word closest in composition to THE tongue itself.

It is one of THE words most foreign to us in our own language. THE is, in fact, a pivotal factor in THE dehumanization of man through THE humanizing influence of language. For example, I may say "I feel that in my blood" using THE language as it has existed up till now, but I may not without incredible distortion say: I feel THE in my blood.

THE is THE archetypal juncture among all modalities.

When THE airplane takes off from THE ground both THEs become more free-wheeling. When THE hand is put in THE box THE two THEs overlap.

When there is a toothache THE is pressed right up against THE boundaries of pain. When illogic is perpetrated on a sentence, THE is capable of THE most fantastic contortions. As *la* and *le,* and as THE in translations of Rimbaud's distortions of THE senses a single THE can be seen to fold in and out of itself, to explain (possibly explode) expand, twist about an uttered axis, nearly completely reverse itself while maintaining THE same meaning or lack thereof.

Once as someone was dying, his last word was almost THE, but instead it was left in a membranous lump during his tenth to last cough.

THE lines THE. THE lines THE perceptions. THE lines THE (don't be afraid) electrical smoke showers of perceptions serving as a buffer and a stop-gap.

A is a fraction of THE. It's probably as interesting.

When I see you next please tell me what THE is, not what it is for. THE is democratic, revolutionary and Marxist as well as elitist, monarchic and fascistic. A wrong word is very different from THE wrong word. THE right word or system is very different from a right word or system. THE is a way which has been battened down.

THE AS IN:

(1) Neither an outside observer nor THE Subject who undergoes THE process can explain fully how particular experiences are able to change one's centre of energy so decisively, or why they so often have to bide their hour to do so.

Varieties of Religious Experience
William James p. 193

(2) THE enlarged sentence, however, allows as a rule of considerable freedom in THE handling of what may be called "unessential" parts.

Language
Edward Sapir p. 37

(3) Peace to THE tomb that lightly lies upon
THE sacred dust of loved Eurymedon

Theocritus or Leonides of Tarentum
Trans. by D.M.P.

(4) THE walls are scal'd; THE rolling flames arise

She paints THE horrors of a conquer'd town
THE heroes slain, THE palaces o'erthrown
THE matrons ravished, THE whole race enslav'd!

Homer Illiad ix
Trans. by Alexander Pope
(THE seems to have been added)

(5) And THE wood rings with Amarillis' name

Virgil (70-19 B.C.) Ecologues i,5
Trans. by Samuel Johnson

(6) Wel wiste he, by THE droghte and by THE reyn
THE yeldynge of his seed and of his greyn.

THE Canterbury Tales
Chaucer

(7) THE blewe a mort uppone THE bent
THE semblyd on sydis shear;
To THE quyrry then THE Perse went
To se THE bryttlynge off THE deare.

Chevy Chase
Anon.

(8) THE other shape, if shape it might be called
that shape had none......

Paradise Lost
John Milton (1608– 1674)

(9) For instance, simple diving, either by one or both birds, without any fetching of weed from THE bottom, is introduced as part of THE courtship between THE two bouts of shaking.

THE Courtship Habits of THE Great Crested Grebe
Julian Huxley p. 52

(10) If semi-legendary Hengist and Horsa had been unable to overcome THE resistance of THE Romanized Britons and had been hurled back into THE North Sea, this language we today call English might have been as Romance as French or

as Celtic as Welsh, and might have been known by another name besides. If THE charge of Harold's men at Hastings had not been broken by THE showers of Norman arrows raining from THE skies, our tongue today might be as close to German as it is Dutch, or closer.

THE Story of English
Mario Pei p. 7

(11) In normal visual fixation, THE image that falls on THE retina is never really stable; physiological mystagmus,! THE continuous tremor of THE normal eye at rest, causes a slight but constant variation in THE rods and cones that are excited.

Visual Perception Approached by THE Method of Stabilized Images
R.M. Pritchard, Woodburn Heron and D.O. Hebb p. 191
Perception edited by Paul

(12) THE Phenomena were roused.

Illuminations
Rimbaud—Louise Varese p. 133

(13) ...THE original action is THE same as with THE copper chloride solution but a secondary reaction takes place on account of THE activity of THE sodium. THE chlorine escapes as before.

THE Story of Chemistry
Hippolyte Gruener p. 130

(14) THE darkness inside THE taxi slid and swayed as quarters, halves and whole squares of ashen light passed from window to window.

Laughter in THE Dark
Nabokov p. 32

(15) THE fact is I have talked and laughed enough for years instead of weeks, so my memory is quite confounded with THE noise.

Letter to W.D. Fox
Charles Darwin, November

There are as many THEs as there are nouns or options to become nouns. No, there are more. Every THE is a translation. Some translations are very sloppy, others are too poetic, too rigorous or too loud. Some THEs can be translated perfectly into other THEs, others cannot. Although THE length of THE sound of each THE is usually within THE domain of THE individual speaker, at times circumstances will force this (THE) out of his control.

Roughly (and tumultuously) categories into which THE might fall are THE Vast, THE semi-Vast and THE Pinioned.

Two examples of Vast THEs can be found side by side in:

"THE Subject who undergoes THE process..."

[William James—(1) in the above]

THE is also Vast in THE Milton (8):

THE other shape, if shape it might be called
that shape had none...

There are in THE selection from *THE Story of English* [Mario Pei—(10)] both Vast and semi-Vast THEs; THE first THE in THE phrase "THE resistance of THE Romanized Britons..." is Vast, while THE second one can be seen to be only semi-Vast. The third and fourth and sixth THEs of this paragraph are also Vast; these are, respectively, THE North Sea...THE charge of Harold's men...; and THE skies..."—while THE of "THE showers of Norman arrows", of a lesser, rather more finite, order, is considered merely semi-Vast.

In THE selection from THE Pritchard, Heron and Hebb article on visual perception THE domain of "THE continuous tremor of THE normal eye at rest" is in the first instance vastness (that is, as long as such movement is considered to be immeasurable) and in the second instance not more than semi-Vast (some would say Pinioned, but see later).

It is a question of what THE is called upon to carry. Almost nothing is left out of what it must carry in Rimbaud's (12) "THE Phenomena were roused."

All vastness as it resides in memory lies in THE final THE of THE Darwin citation:

THE fact is I have talked and laughed enough for weeks instead of years, so my memory is quite confounded with THE noise.

Vast THE will be found to be readily present in ancient text or in translation; in these cases assumed time-space distances give vastness to what would ordinarily be considered only semi-Vast. See (6), (7), [particularly the 2nd and 4th THEs therein], and also, to some degree, (4?) and (5).

Semi-Vast THE is just a bit or quite a bit less; it is really the middle range and is as such ubiquitous, particularly. A few examples should suffice:

In Sapir (2)—"THE enlarged sentence, however, allows as a rule considerable freedom in THE handling of what may be called 'unessential' parts", both THEs handle large but not untameably vast areas.

Disregarding time and translation, for the sake of establishing a definition, could we not say that THE second THE in the following quotation has an extensive but limited range and is therefore nothing other than semi-Vast?

"Peace to THE tomb that lightly lies upon THE sacred dust of loved Eurymedon."

Theocritus or Leonides of Tarentum

These THEs: "THE bottom" and "Simple diving... is introduced as part of THE courtship between THE two bouts of shaking" [J. Huxley—(9)] work up a semi-Vast domain.

The first of the following two THEs is semi-Vast: "THE darkness inside THE taxi [Nabokov— (14)]

THE transpiring of a certain qualified vastness:

...THE original action is THE same as with THE copper chloride solution but a secondary reaction takes place on account of THE sodium. THE chlorine escapes as before.

THE Story of Chemistry
Hippolyte Gruener

One way of reading this description is to find THE repeatedly bringing us back to THE as a or THE substratum of THE action, but a more even reading of it reveals THE catalytic action of THE, THE specificity of its range, its semi- rather than its full-blown Vastness.

Actually some might say that our very first example of Vast THE can equally well be regarded as semi-Vast:

Neither an outside observer nor THE Subject who undergoes THE process can explain fully how particular experiences are able to change one's centre of energy so decisively, or why they so often have to bide their hour to do so..

It is not always easy to know where to draw THE line. THE slides this continuum.

THE last to be discussed category is THE Pinioned THE; THE as place marker or small reflector. Some examples of this category found in the present group of citations are: THE taxi; THE retina; THE fact; THE rods and cones. Some might designate THE THE of THE image to be a simple pinioning, but I find it semi-Vast if not Vast in its complexity. After all, even THE text in which it here appears tells us that "THE image that falls on THE retina is never really stable." I doubt such an image can be pinned down. Similarly, ostensibly Pinioned, "THE wood [which] rings with Amarillis' name" resonates vastly, semi-.

As suggested before, THE crossing of centuries and languages may turn even a Pinioned THE Vast; THE as THE root of THE matter lifted in this way suddenly Heavenwards, out from where it is, becomes, at a moment's notice, Vast. To know this pleasure turn once again to THE specimens of THE in quotations nos. (6) and (7) and give these THEs full play.

(THE) out of his control.

Depending on circumstances THE magnificence or debasement of any THE may be simply reversed. THE longest THE on record was emitted during an epileptic fit in which THE conscious matrix became associated with an acidic ice water made of sound. In order to counteract its sometimes limp nature, THE word THE is often infused with THE word 'for' or is projected out around THE core concept of 'force'.

THE may be found at every vertex of a triangle. Neither will it be absent in this century from almost any interstices. It is one of THE most redundant terms in THE English language. It need not be said. It may or may not have been thought, but once it has been structured into a language, it implies itself continuously.

A motorcar pulled up to THE bridge. A young man walked out of THE car. THE young man was holding a paper bag. THE paper bag was placed beside a tree. This was in Grenada. A sun shone through THE branches of THE tree. THE sun moved behind a cloud. THE cloud moved. THE sun shone on THE paper bag as well as on THE tree and THE ground. THE ground was wet. A path led to a farmhouse, THE path did not lead straight to THE farmhouse. It stopped by a lake. THE lake was between THE man and THE farmhouse.

THE zooms in on A; it intensifies and firms out; it is capable of suggesting traction. THE formula for making THE adjustment from indefinite to definite article is:

From A to THE

$$A^2 + E + Mx - pi^4 + Wx\ Th + 98^0(\pm)\ 6 = THE$$

If this is not comprehensible it is wrong.

Most creative masterpieces (?) are expressions of THE: either (depending on THE society) an homage to its presence or THE fulfilling of its role in its absence. When you are looking at any painting, it is not just any painting, it is THE painting at which you are looking. Though this may seem like quibbling, it is THE largest scale quibbling of which we know. There are now: THE style, THE media, THE content. Any work of art, as a record of decisions, a particularizing of taste, is, when exhibited, what THE artist wanted THE painting (music, book) to be: then, it becomes THE expression of a new (imitative, combinative) *THE.* Duchamp takes a urinal and makes it THE urinal (though still with lovely revolutionary overtones of A) by virtue of its placement in THE gallery. In all this, THE is not simply an article which particularizes (and this article is not just an attempt to generalize the use of particularization) nor does it ever truly lose its body which is THE word THE with all its sound, weight, and familiarity. Yet it is THE mnemonic device for: THE moment at which mystery opaques; THE devising of mnemonic devices; THE stuffing of as many firmaments as possible into THE diachronic headlines; any art or piece of it.

As many ways as a meat loaf or a roast beef may be thought to be able to be cut or broken off, those are equal to or less than THE number of THE's which may be pressed into service under those conditions.

It is foolish to sway: THE stood on THE bridge and then jumped with all its might.

In time this THE will disappear. Perhaps it is without a doubt that another THE will surface. THE is a lover. It is a diagonal (not always) line through an energy soup. (Forget it) I wonder just how erasable it is. A kiss to those who've finished this article.

The President Reacts

There are a few inaccuracies.

I don't like the quality of paper which was used. Was this really printed by Alger Hiss?

Why has this nothing to do with me?

I would...

I think my name is misspelt.

This book is much worse than war!

Not everything in the book has been fully covered.

I am surprised that no mention was made of my singing voice.

It made me very, very sad.

For everyone!

This book is as good as the war!

Bearded luck!

Hold it! Read it! Stampede it! Not to be missed!

If Karl Marx were Madeline Gins, he would have written this!

I don't mind anything except the fact that my penis was mentioned several times.

I couldn't get completely through it because of the bloody pages.

This is too religious for me.

Almost too pointless.

A little disappointed, having expected a real thriller.

I loved and hated every other minute of it.

I couldn't have done it better myself—so much the worse for her.

It has given me a reason to live... now that I have the scent...

Stay away from this if you are either near-souled or far-souled, critically speaking.

Exquisitely purposeless!

This book was
designed by Susan Quasha
and typeset in Perpetua
at Open Studio by Vicki Fein.
Twenty-six copies have been
lettered and signed by the author.